Unblinking

MADE IN MICHIGAN WRITERS SERIES

GENERAL EDITORS

Michael Delp, Interlochen Center for the Arts

M. L. Liebler, Wayne State University

A complete listing of the books in this series can be found online
at wsupress.wayne.edu

Un blinking

Stories by Lisa Lenzo

WAYNE STATE UNIVERSITY PRESS
DETROIT

ISBN 978-0-8143-4671-6 (paperback)
ISBN 978-0-8143-4672-3 (e-book)

Library of Congress Control Number: 2018957218

Publication of this book was made possible by a generous gift from The Meijer Foundation. This work is supported in part by an award from the Michigan Council for Arts and Cultural Affairs.

Wayne State University Press
Leonard N. Simons Building
4809 Woodward Avenue
Detroit, Michigan 48201-1309

Visit us online at wsupress.wayne.edu

For my sibs,
Steve, Peter, Kris, Anthony, and Amy,
and our mom and dad,
Susie and Joe

Contents

⊙

In the White Man's House

Back in the day, the two of us were tight; people rattled off our names, "Tremaine-and-Jay," as if we couldn't be split apart. That began to change in tenth grade, when Jay started calling his parents—not to their faces, but to me—"the light, *right* Negroes" and "Dr. and Mrs. Tom."

We'd stop over at Jay's house after school, and the minute we'd walk in the door, his face would twist into a scowl. "Look at this carpet!" he would demand. I'd look at the carpet. It was thick and soft and the color of cream—a shade lighter than Jay's pale beige skin—and it ran through their whole downstairs except for the kitchen. "It's sick!" Jay would say. "Damn honky-ass rug." Then, still scowling, he'd shout, "Mama! You home?"

He knew that she wasn't, he was just making sure. He'd stand there in the foyer, chewing on the tip of his middle finger. Then he'd tromp through the living room and on into the dining room and reach up and break off a little piece of the chandelier. It was one of those chandeliers made of hundreds of prisms of glass, and he'd just reach up his hand and snap off a piece. Sometimes he'd have to give it a yank, or take out his pocketknife and saw through the connecting wire. Then he'd slip the little prism into his pocket. You couldn't tell anything was missing from the chandelier unless you knew or looked close, but if he kept it up, sooner or later, it was going to get noticed—probably by Gladys, their maid, when she stepped up to dust.

But Jay didn't care, or else maybe he couldn't help himself. He was so embarrassed by his family: his father the doctor, his sister the scholar, his mother the high-yellow, high-society homemaker. He'd have liked to load the chandelier, Gladys, and his family into their Mercedes, then push them off the Ambassador Bridge.

I wished I had his kind of problem. Our house was falling apart, inside and out, and my mom, whose dark brown skin Jay admired, was so depressed that she'd barely glance at the bills when they came in—she'd just add them to the pile. My mom was working, but only part-time, serving lunch at my sister's school. Then she'd come home and sleep all afternoon. My super-light-skinned dad had left us when I was ten and my little sister was six. He'd taken up with a white woman and vanished into the white world. I had a job after school and on weekends busing tables and washing dishes, having become, by default, the man of the house. Yet Jay envied my family because to him—except for my passing-for-white dad—we were "blacker" than his.

Around the time Jay started carving up his mother's chandelier, he traded his pocketknife for a switchblade and bought a shiny green suit. One night he came over to my house wearing this new suit with a gold shirt and chewing on a chicken leg. My girlfriend and I had been listening to *Let's Get It On* and making out on the couch. Melanie and I pulled apart when Jay walked in, but I kept my hand on her thigh so she'd stay on my lap.

I'd met Mel at my job, five months back. She came in with a couple of her black girlfriends, and at first I thought she was a black girl herself. Her skin was light, but her brown hair was curly and short, and she talked and acted as if she were black. She's one of those borderline people, like my dad: if you set them next to white people, they look white, and if they're hanging with black people, you assume they are black. I thought Mel might be mixed—I guessed her mother might be white—but I found out later that her father was white, too. They lived south of Six Mile, in the city of Highland Park, which is bordered all the way around by Detroit.

Jay sat down next to me and Mel on the couch without saying *Hey* or *What's up?* Instead he worked away at that drumstick he'd carried in, ripping off the meat in chunks. He scraped the leg bare with his teeth, sucked on the bone, then tossed it on the floor.

Mel and I looked at each other; I could read her face like she could read mine: *What's with the superfly suit? And throwing bones on the floor—was that supposed to be some kind of down-home black thing?*

Jay just sat there without explaining, like he wore a green suit and a gold shirt and tossed bones around every day.

I cleared my throat and asked, "Uh, Jay—what's your problem?"

"What do you mean?" Jay said, kind of innocent but tough.

I pointed at the bone and said, "What I mean is, what's up with that?"

Jay looked down at the chicken bone resting by his shiny black boots. "Ain't nothin' but a bone."

"You don't throw bones on the floor at your house."

"This more my house than that place," Jay grumbled.

"Well, do me a favor, then, and put that bone where it belongs."

Jay picked up the bone, but instead of carrying it out to the can in the kitchen, he shoved it into his suit pocket and mumbled something about me "talkin' too white."

"Well, I am part white," I said. "I'm part Cherokee, too. I could be sitting around talking Cherokee. Then you wouldn't even understand me."

"You know what I mean, Tremaine," Jay said. "This ain't about *comprehension*. It's about you not respectin' *our people*."

"Which people?" I said, staring at Jay's light face and his half inch of straight hair. He obviously had a white ancestor or two, and even though my own hair is nappy and my skin is a deep brown, half of my blood comes from my dad, who was so able and willing to pass that he passed right out of our lives. Back then, in 1975, my mom and sister and I hadn't seen my dad in five years. Now it's been over forty. I don't even know whether he is still alive.

I don't know if Jay is alive, either.

"Fuck you, Tremaine," Jay said. "You just like my parents. Proud to be house slaves. Forgettin' who they are so long as they get to live in the white man's big house!"

"Jaybird, your parents live in their own damn big house," I said.

"Shit," Jay said, "them *and* their house belong to white folks. The white man owns everything and everyone in this country."

"Well, if we're *all* owned by the white man," I said, "then why are you so down on your folks?"

" 'Cause they *like* being owned," Jay said. " 'Cause they sold themselves out for a mansion and a Mercedes."

Mel ducked her head near mine and whispered, "Jaybird think he the next Malcolm X."

Jay heard her, and he lit right into her: "Don't be callin' me Jaybird!"

"You don't say nothin' to Tree when *he* call you Jaybird," Mel objected.

"And if you wasn't here," Jay said, "I wouldn't say nothin' to you."

"Man, do you know how sick I am of this shit?" Mel said, strapping her arms across her breasts. Ever since Jay had got onto his "the-blacker-the-better" kick, Melanie had become Jay's number one enemy. He thought she was undermining my blackness—maybe even ruining my black soul.

"You guys want to do something?" I asked. Mel was up on her feet and stalking around; no chance she'd return to my lap until she calmed down, and that wouldn't happen with Jay scowling at her, which was the main way he looked at pretty much everyone anymore. "Like maybe go for a ride?" I said.

"Long as we got a car tonight?" Mel had recently got her license, along with the use of her parents' car. But Mel and Jay acted like they didn't even hear me.

"Why don't you get your *own* self a girlfriend," Mel said, "and stop worrying about what ain't none of your business?"

"It *is* my business," Jay said. "Tree's my best friend."

"And he is *my boyfriend*," Mel shot back. "And ain't nothin' you can do about it."

Mel had hung with black boyfriends and girlfriends ever since Highland Park started to turn. I guess that's part of why I liked her so much: she didn't *have to* throw in, heart and soul, with black people; she chose us. Jay felt the opposite: she was white; she should stay out of our lives. This led to a lot of fights, with me right in the middle.

"You ain't gonna stick with him," Jay said. "You gonna drop him like a burnt potato and take up with some ugly-ass white boy."

"I don't even know any white boys," Mel growled, still stalking around. She jammed her hand into her pocket, pulled out a stick of gum, unwrapped it, and shoved it into her mouth.

"There be white boys at your school," Jay said.

"Shit," Mel said. "About fifteen. 'Bout fifteen white boys, and a thousand black men."

"A thousand!" I said. "Damn, I guess I'm lucky I made the cut!" I was trying to make Mel smile and at least soften Jay's frown, but neither of them even looked in my direction.

"So why don't you go with one of them fifteen white boys?" Jay asked.

"Because," Mel said, "there ain't one I even *like*."

"Why not?" Jay asked. "Why don't you like white boys?"

"'Cause they're a bunch of scared rabbits. And anyway, I'm all the way in love with Tremaine."

I would have pulled her down and kissed her if Jay weren't there, but I didn't want to make him jealous. He hadn't had a girlfriend, black or white, in six months. He claimed the black girls at Mumford, where we went to school, weren't black enough. Not even the darkest ones.

"Let's go somewhere," I sighed. I didn't feel like sitting around refereeing all night.

"I'm broke," Jay said.

I wanted to say, *We could cut down what's left of your mom's chandelier and hock it.* I wished things were the way they used to be, when we could joke about anything.

"We could go to the playoffs," Mel said. "They're free."

"What playoffs?" I asked.

"Between Highland Park and Dearborn," Mel said. "They playing at the fairgrounds tonight."

"No shit," I said. "You didn't tell me that."

Mel shrugged. "We make it to the top every year in basketball, 'cause they lump us in with the suburbs. Every year we get our asses kicked in swimming, but in basketball, can't nobody touch us. Only this year, we playing Dearborn, and people be saying them Arab boys is tough."

"Hell, let's go then," I said.

I figured Jay wouldn't want to be seen with us, but he decided to come along and watch Highland Park play. Considering his new logic, I'm sure he thought Highland Park was a cooler school than ours. Both were nearly all black, but

Highland Park was poorer than Mumford, and to Jay, poorer meant blacker.

⊙

The minute we stepped out the door, Jay's face took on a moodier look—a scowl instead of a frown. He wouldn't sit up in the front of the station wagon with Mel and me, but slouched down in the back, chewing on his middle finger, his other hand shoved into his suit coat pocket, feeling on a piece of chandelier or chicken bone, I guessed, or maybe that switchblade of his. I knew he was worrying about showing up in a black place with Melanie, being seen with a white girl by a bunch of bloods.

I went to turn the radio on, then drew back my hand. Mel's parents weren't poor, but like a lot of white people, they were cheap, and in their new Chrysler wagon, there was just a flat, blue piece of plastic covering the slot where the radio should be. When we first discovered this sad lack was the only time I heard Mel curse her parents, under her breath.

Mel backed out of the driveway and drove the two blocks north from my house to Eight Mile. "The Mile," people called it, as if there were no other mile roads. Eight Mile was wider than Seven and Six, but more important, it was the dividing line between Detroit and the suburbs, the designated border between black and white, an eight-lane street blacks weren't supposed to cross. Mel drove north to The Mile, turned east, and took it over to Woodward, then drove south on Woodward to the fairground entrance.

I don't know whose idea it was to build the state fairgrounds right in the city of Detroit. I never questioned it as a kid, though I did think it a strange place when my mom or auntie took me there. I'd go on a couple rides, then walk around gawking at all the white farmers and their cows. They also had weird chickens with mops of feathers growing out of their little heads, and humongous pigs with what seemed like twenty teats, but the strangest and most disturbing thing I ever saw at the fair was a man in the freak tent who was called "the frog boy."

He was a light-skinned black man with a deformed body and a normal head. In my memory, his face looks exactly like Malcolm X's—maybe because of the glasses he wore, his red-toned complexion, and the intelligence of his expression. His body was on the small side, and he had these little, tiny arms drawn up close to his chest. His legs were small and deformed, too, but bigger than his arms. He was squatting on the ground with his legs bent outward and double like a frog's. He squatted there, describing to the audience his "half-frog, half-boy" body and life, and as I listened to him talk—in this deep, fake, bullfrog voice—it was so obviously a bunch of crap; in two seconds flat I could see he was in no way part frog. Likely the only true thing he said was that he was thirty-three years old.

I left that tent without stopping to look at the other freaks, not even the white Siamese twins, which was what I'd gone in to see. When I came out into the daylight my auntie looked at me and laughed. "What's wrong with you, Tree?" she said. "Something in there scare you?"

That night I couldn't sleep because I kept thinking of my father. My mother had tracked him down a year ago. She took me along with her, somewhere north of Eight Mile, where the houses sat far back from the street and the lawns looked soft enough to sleep on. We walked up the stone steps of a big house in this rich neighborhood. My mom rang the bell—a fancy chime, not a ring or a buzz—and a white woman with a brown mole on her chin answered the door. My mom asked to speak to Josh Logan, and my dad came up behind the white woman and said, "I'll take care of this, Lois."

He came out onto the front porch, closing the door firmly behind him. I think my mom and I were the only ones in that whole suburb who knew he wasn't a white man. He gave my mom all the money in his wallet—a bunch of twenties and some ones—and said he would send her a check soon. He told her not to come there again, but to call him on the phone next time she needed anything. I was eleven years old then and tall enough to look him in the eye. But he only glanced at me once and then looked away without smiling. His dark hair was straight—what black people used to call "good hair"—and his eyes were large and hazel and shining with fear. Despite my brown skin and nappy hair, I looked a lot like him: same thin lips and broad cheeks, same big, gold-flecked eyes that showed what I was feeling. I hadn't seen my dad since before Christmas, when he left for work one day and just never came home. I wanted to sidle up close to his chest, feel his big hand come to rest on my shoulder. But he stepped backwards into the house and shut the heavy front door. My mom went alone another time to see him, but he was gone—a real white man and his family were living in that big house.

I never saw the "frog boy" again, either. After I left the freak tent, I wandered around, but I couldn't keep my mind on the rides or the animals. I wanted to go back in and tell that man to stop lying, to stop pretending to be something he wasn't. The following year, I stayed away from that part of the fair, and the year after that, all the freak shows had been banished—it wasn't okay anymore to stare at people because they looked different.

Since then I've had dreams of walking into a freak tent and seeing my father under the lights: a tall, handsome man who can shift, in an instant, from black into white. Sometimes my little sister is standing beside him, her nappy blond hair flowing over her shoulders, her light, gray-blue eyes as soft as the sky.

⊙

On the night of the playoffs, which were held in mid-March, the fairgrounds were a completely different place than they were in late summer. It was dark and cold, the wind whipping up dust, and the buildings seemed more than temporarily abandoned—they looked so forgotten and deserted, it seemed as if no one would ever use them again. The only light came from the arena and its parking lot, which was separated from the rest of the fairgrounds by a tall chain-link fence topped by strands of barbed wire. Only a few cars were parked inside the fence, and no people were in sight.

"You sure they holding it here?" I asked Mel.

"Yeah," Mel said. "Ain't hardly any cars 'cause most people come by bus. See, what they do is, they rent a bunch of buses, and then after the game, Highland Park go out the doors on *their* side and pile on *their* buses, and the other team go out the doors on *their* side and pile on *their* buses, and that way, nobody gets in each other's faces."

Melanie had stopped the station wagon about a hundred feet back from the closed gate. "You can come in your own car if you want," she said, tapping the steering wheel with her red-polished fingernails, each of which was divided by a thunderbolt decal. "Mostly nobody drive in their own car from Dearborn, I suppose cause they too afraid to be drivin' over here, and mostly nobody drive in their own car from Highland Park because, for one, mostly nobody have a car, and for two, whoever ride on the buses get in free."

"I thought you said it was free regardless," Jay said.

Mel turned around and stared into the back seat. "Don't tell me you don't got two dollars in that fancy coat."

Before Jay could answer, I said, "I got extra."

We stepped out of the station wagon, walked across the asphalt, and slipped through the space between the two halves of the tall gate. It felt like we were sneaking into a prison, only there weren't any guards.

Inside the stadium was a big crowd, or really, two big crowds: at least a hundred, all white, including a sprinkling of Arabs, on the Dearborn side, and about two hundred, all black, on the side for Highland Park. The game was in the beginning of the third quarter, and Highland Park was leading, 28 to 23. If anyone had been collecting money at the door, they had stopped. Nobody was selling refreshments, either. I saw an empty block of seats about halfway up on the Highland Park side and motioned for Jay and Mel to follow me. I didn't take Mel's hand and was careful to not brush against her. I always held back from touching her in public whatever kind of crowd we were in, black or white or some of each. I had noticed that sex between blacks and whites, real or imagined, made racism burn hotter. And it didn't fire up only white people's tempers—it fired up black folks, too.

As we started up the steps between the rows of seats, Mel waved to someone high in the stands, her hand arcing back and forth like a windshield wiper on high, her smile spread all the way across her pretty face. I reminded myself that she went to school with this crowd every day.

We sat down, and out of the corner of my eye I saw something moving. I glanced up. Mel, looking up to the highest bleachers, was signaling to her friends, her thunderbolt pointer finger nailing the air near my head: *This is him—my boyfriend.* I was pleased, but still I said, "Mel, stop attracting attention."

"Oh, you gettin' bad as Jay," Mel said.

I looked around for Jay. He was sitting in the row in front of us, off to my right, acting like he hadn't come with us. He looked strange to me in that bright green suit and his shiny black boots; used to be all he wore were dull-colored T-shirts, jeans, and high-tops. "Hey, Slim, do I know you from somewhere?" I asked. He didn't respond, so I leaned over and prodded his shoulder. Jay turned around slowly and just looked at me without speaking, his eyes full of misery and pleading. Then he faced forward again. I unzipped my jacket and settled back to watch the game.

All of Highland Park's players were black, and all of Dearborn's were white—if you considered Arabs white, which everyone did back then, at least in Detroit, even though most Arabs were as dark as Mexicans. On Dearborn's team, the Arabs were the stars. They weren't as tall as their lighter white teammates or the Highland Park players, but they were quick on their feet and aggressive. There was a lot of bumping and shoving going on, but very few fouls were being called—one referee was white and one was black, and neither wanted to get mixed up in anyone's business any more than they had to.

The game stayed close, with Highland Park always between one and four points ahead. Then, as Kendall Jewel, Highland Park's leading scorer, was driving in for a layup, a big white boy slammed into him, and Kendall Jewel went down hard. Everybody on the Highland Park side leapt to their feet. I was up before I knew it, trying to see what was going on, wordless cries mixed with swear words flying from my mouth. The crowd all around us was roaring with anger and disbelief. Someone near us said, "You see what that motherfuckin' honky did?"

A foul was called, and Highland Park announced a timeout. Down on the court, several Highland Park players were blocking a tall, long-armed teammate who was trying to reach the big, brawny white boy who'd laid out Kendall Jewel. "The Jewel" was lying motionless, flat on the floor, with the coach kneeling beside him. Then Kendall picked himself up and walked stiffly to the bench. The game started up again without him and, not long after, Dearborn made two shots and pulled into the lead. At the top of our stands, a group started to chant: *"We the best, you know it's true! Gonna kick your ass when the game is through!"*

The chant spread up and down our side of the stadium. I looked around to see if the teachers or principals would do anything about it. At Mumford's games, there were always a few adults—teachers and parents and also the principal and vice p—scattered among the students. But I didn't see any adults in the stands here, except for one man dressed in a super-fly suit like Jay's—only his suit was orange, and he was up on his feet and chanting like a wild man. There were no cheerleaders, either, at least none who were official. About fifteen girls without uniforms—some in skirts, some in pants—were standing on the wooden bleacher seats at the top of the stadium, dancing and clapping a beat to the chant: *"We the best! You know it's true! Gonna kick your ass when the game is through!"*

I didn't join in the chant, and neither did Jay or Mel. Jay was facing straight ahead, as subdued as Kendall Jewel; Mel was admiring some skinny dark girl's new baby. Mel held the baby with both palms and gave it a heft. "Girl, you laid yourself a brick!" she said. "Tree, check out this big baby." I looked at the fat, light-skinned baby and smiled. He would grow darker—"ripe up," my grandma called it—as he grew older. Though my grandma had said that about my sister, and Laura never did. There's not a trace of black visible in my sister except in her hair, which is kinky but dark blond, and in her lips and her nose, which are a bit broad for a white girl. Whoever made up the rules on race—*This is black, that is white*—was messed up.

The chanting continued until Highland Park pulled into the lead again. Then, when they fell behind, another chant started: *"When you're hot, you're hot! When you're not, you're not! Gonna kick your ass in the parking lot!"* Kendall Jewel was back in the game. The chanting seemed to keep getting louder. The bleacher seats clattered and trembled with stomps.

In the middle of all this commotion, someone behind us clapped his hands over Mel's eyes—white hands, I saw. I looked up into this greasy white dude's face as Mel peeled the hands from her eyes and turned around. "Dean!" she cried out. "What you doing here?"

"Come to watch Highland Park kick some ass," the white dude said. Mel smiled at him, then looked at me. "Dean, this is my boyfriend, Tremaine."

Just then another white dude walked up. While Dean's hair was short and slicked back, this man, older than Dean, had long blond hair parted down the middle and divided into two braids. It was a style like you'd see on a white girl or an Indian, and besides those two head braids, the man's *beard* was braided—he had three short blond braids that stuck straight down from his chin.

"Bobby!" Mel shouted, grinning wide. She stood up and gave this weird person a hug. "I thought you was in Alaska."

"I was in Alaska," Bobby said, smiling back. "But now I'm here." Mel, still grinning, started the introductions over, this time trying to include Jay. But when she called to him, he turned around and grimaced in our direction without making eye contact, then turned back to the court, hunched up in his green suit coat like a turtle. I knew the last thing Jay wanted was to meet a couple of white dudes, especially one with three braids sticking down from his chin.

Bobby and Dean, who turned out to be brothers, sat down right behind us. Whenever the game got exciting, the white brothers leapt up and shook their fists in the air and shouted. They even joined in on the chanting: *"When you're hot, you're hot! When you're not, you're not! Gonna kick your ass in the parking lot!"*

"They don't go to your school, do they?" I asked Mel, remembering she'd said all the white boys were scared rabbits. And also, these guys looked too old for high school.

"Not anymore," Mel said. "Dean got out about two or

three years ago, and Bobby's been out for even longer. He used to have short hair like his brother, but then he went over to Vietnam, and when he got back, he was totally different."

"Yeah, no kidding," I said. I could understand having two head braids if he was part Indian or something, but three blond *beard* braids? That didn't seem to make sense on any kind of a person.

"They live a couple blocks over from me," Mel said. "Now Dean's a fireman for Highland Park, and Bobby, he's a handyman, plus he drives old women home from the store for a couple bucks." She leaned close to me and said right next to my ear, "He looks kind of crazy, but really, he's not. Vietnam made a lot of guys mean, but it did the opposite to Bobby—it made him more peaceful. Dean says Bobby won't get drunk and raise hell with him no more, he just smokes weed and kicks back."

"Looks to me like he could still raise some hell," I said. Bobby was on his feet again, chanting, thrusting his fist straight up like he was punching a ceiling. The few other people still chanting were seated, except for the girls dancing at the top of the bleachers. There were at least twenty dancing up there, laughing, having a good time. The wooden seats rumbled and thumped like drums with their measured stomping. I turned back to the game and watched the players sweep up and down the court.

⊙

It stayed close all the way to the end, but Highland Park finally won, 52 to 50. The kids on the Dearborn side filed out of their exits quietly, heads down, drifting along their aisles like ghosts in a hurry. Some Highland Parkers were laughing and calling out happily, but others were still angry about that white boy slamming into Kendall Jewel. "Someone should slam *his* ass in the parking lot," a short boy said.

"We should knock them *all* on their asses," another Parker answered.

"Lucky they on the other side of this building," a third Parker said. He cupped his hands to his mouth: "Run on off to the suburbs, you white chickens! You not cool enough to live in the city!"

Mel had turned around in her seat to talk with Bobby while we waited for the crowd to thin. Even while I listened to the mix of angry and happy chatter of the folks passing out of the stands, I couldn't keep my eyes from Bobby's face—I was drawn to those three freaky braids jutting down from his chin. But I made myself look at the rest of his face, too. Behind his wire-rimmed glasses, his eyes were clear and cool.

When the building was half empty, we got up and left. Bobby and Dean walked out right ahead of the three of us. There were no buses on our side—they hadn't showed up yet, I guessed. The people standing around us waiting for the buses were all from Highland Park. The Dearborn crowd was on the other side of the arena, so except for Dean, Bobby, and Mel, there were no white people in sight.

The white brothers and Jay and Mel and I started walking toward the gate. We'd only taken a few steps when I heard someone behind us say, "How'd *they* get over *here*?" And then someone else: "What *they* doin' on *our* side?" They were speaking loudly on purpose, to make sure we heard them.

Although the night was cold, the air behind us seemed to

thicken with a kind of heat. I kept walking, Mel by my side. I couldn't think of anything else to do. Bobby and Dean were straight in front of us, Jay a little farther up ahead—trying to put some distance, I figured, between him and the white brothers and Mel. Some quieter Highland Park students were walking to the side of us and in front, and they didn't seem to notice anything going on.

I tried to walk at a normal pace, not too fast or too slow, I tried to pretend that nothing was happening behind us. Because I knew if I acted like I wasn't afraid, if I acted like things were all right, that's how things most likely would go. At least I hoped so.

The parking lot lights shone down on us. Dean, Bobby, and Mel showed up more in that light than I did, and so did Jay, with his close-to-white skin. My own brown skin blended in with the night. It also blended in with the crowd. If I took two steps to the side, no one would know who I'd come with; I could just disappear. I could slip off and melt into that same-colored crowd, like my father had done.

My hearing seemed sharper walking in front of that revved-up throng, as if I could pick up the slightest sound. I heard coat sleeves rustling and feet shuffling, sharp laughter and soft voices whose words I couldn't make out—and beneath all these noises, I felt a fast, silent humming, silent and electric, racing through the air and the people behind me and throughout my whole body.

Just then I heard a loud bang—it sounded like a gun going off. Bobby looked over his shoulder as if someone behind him had called his name. His head was tipped slightly back as he surveyed the crowd, his eyes narrowed and piercing, glasses catching the light, and his blond beard braids jutted like spikes from his chin.

"Not *them*," a voice said from behind us. And then another voice spoke, right next to my ear: "Not them—they're from Highland Park."

But Jay apparently didn't hear what they said. I guess all he heard was that loud bang like a shot, because he took off, sprinting in his black boots, his green suit coat sleeves pumping, the back of his jacket shining under the parking lot lights.

Two bloods in jeans and high-tops started to chase him, imitating his arm-pumping, high-stepping stride. But they were just joking; they quickly circled back. Several others were kicking at a garbage can lying on its side—that's what'd made the loud bang, someone knocking the can over. A few people were laughing at the can rattling and rolling around, spewing trash like a knocked-over white boy spilling his guts, and some were laughing at Jay for taking off like a track star after the starting gun. A girl with a loud voice said, "What's that Negro running from?"

But Jay didn't hear that, either, I'm sure; he was too far gone by then. The chain-link and barbed-wire gate had been thrown open, and he passed through it and kept going, racing on past Mel's car, running off into the dark fairgrounds between the stadium and Woodward Avenue.

We drove around for ten minutes before we found him. We spotted him on Woodward, walking along the half-dark street like he knew where he was going, like he had somewhere else to go besides home with us.

⊙

Jay took off for real two years later—he totally disappeared—but by then I'd already lost track of him. Not long after the playoffs, his parents pulled him out of Mumford and enrolled him in an all-white prep school in Grosse Pointe, one of Detroit's wealthiest suburbs. I heard he dropped out before the year was through. I'm not sure what he did with himself after that, before he went missing.

For almost three years, no one knew where Jay was. His father finally found him living on the streets in Chicago and brought him home. He was diagnosed with schizophrenia, which is genetic in part, but my sister, who is a therapist now, says living in a big city doubles the risk, and racism and other kinds of conflict also help to bring it on.

The last time I saw Jay, over thirty years ago, he was living in a group home on the west side of Detroit. I didn't have the heart, or maybe it was the guts, to visit him more than once. Looking at his confused eyes and unkempt hair, listening to him ramble on without understanding even half of what he said, I chose to step off—in other words, to disappear. Not that I decided, when I left the visitor room that day, that I wasn't going back. But I never have so far.

I ended up marrying a black woman who is darker than me, and there's no question, color-wise, about our daughters. But my sister has two boys, Eric and Josh, who could pass for white. I love them almost as much as I love my own kids. Josh's nickname among his black classmates is "Whitey." And just the other day, a couple of white kids asked Eric, "What are you?" and "Where are you from?" So the conflict continues. There's more truth than I like to admit in what Jay used to say: in some ways, even today, we are still living in the white man's house—all of us, every single one of us, whether black or white or both.

⊙

On that night we watched the playoffs, after we saw Jay walking down Woodward, Mel pulled the car alongside him, and I rolled down my window. I was going to say something jokey like, "Hey, blood, where do you think you're going?" But he stepped over to us quickly, without saying a word, and remembering how I had almost slunk off myself, I ended up keeping quiet.

Jay got into the back seat with his eyes averted. I faced forward and gazed out the windshield, and we headed back toward my house. To our right were the suburbs; to our left was Detroit. Directly under us was The Mile, cutting between the two sides like a knife, and at the same time holding them together, joining us like a spine. I didn't say a word to Jay or to Mel as we rolled over that road. Because what could I say? Other than what I'm saying now. Mel sighed and tapped her fingernails on the steering wheel. Jay shuffled his shiny boots. The heater blowing warm air was the only other sound in the car.

Up
in the
Air

Last night I sang a new song, a you-done-me-wrong I learned
from Fat Stan, this old bandmate of mine, and Claudine
thinks I stared directly at her during the song's unloving
refrain. If that had been all, she might have let it slide. But
then, during my first break, a woman who'd had a few drinks
leaned over the left wheel of my wheelchair and trailed her
fingers across my chest, while Claudine, with our little girl
on her hip, stood at my other side. I introduced Claudine to
that woman I didn't know: "This is one of my fans—this is my
wife." Claudine looked like she wanted to spit. The woman
continued to stroke my chest. If I'd pulled back on my wheel
rims, she'd have fallen across my legs; if I'd pushed forward,
I'd have run over her foot. "Oh! I'm so sorry you're married,"
she said, and then she leaned in even closer, lips aiming for my
face. "Well," I told her, grinning like an idiot, "I kind of like

being married." She murmured, "That's too bad," and kissed the side of my head.

After the show, lying in bed in our camper, Claudine said, "For the rest of my life, I'm going to have this picture of that woman's slitty eyes and her slutty lips and you smirking like a jackass and saying you 'kind of' like being married."

I wanted to explain that I'd forget that woman by tomorrow if Claudine would. I wanted to convince my wife beyond a doubt of my love for her, but I couldn't figure out how to say it right then without sounding corny or false. Suddenly the incident seemed as absurd to me as when it was happening, so I said, "Claude, if you forget about being jealous, don't you think the whole thing was kind of funny?"

Claudine clamped her lips and turned her back to me.

⊙

Ten hours later, in the middle of Iowa cornfields, Claude looked up from *One Hundred Years of Solitude* and called me a conceited airhead and an uncaring jerk. I glanced in the rearview to check if Lucy had heard. She'd fallen asleep in her car seat, her binky clutched in her little fist.

"Do you wish you were single again?" Claudine asked, turning in the shotgun seat and frowning at me. "Well, don't let me stop you," she said before I could answer. "You can drop us off when we get to Illinois."

"What would you do in Illinois?" I asked, to pretend that her anger wasn't bothering me and because I was curious. Claudine doesn't know anybody in Illinois—we're both from Detroit—and she doesn't make friends as easily as I do. "The same thing I'd do in any other damn state," Claudine said.

"Get a real job, instead of following you all over the country. I'd stay at home and make dinner every night."

"You'd run out of things to serve," I said. Claudine's basically a breakfast cook.

"People work around those kinds of things," Claudine said.

"They work around these kinds of things, too," I pointed out.

"If they think it's worth it," Claudine said. Then, lifting her long legs and bending them at the knee, she pressed her feet to the dashboard and found her place in *One Hundred Years of Solitude*, which she'd downloaded from the Internet from a list of great books. Claude's read about five so far, parts of them out loud to me. I like hearing the stories, and I love listening to her voice. Mainly because it's hers, but also because she reads like an actor. But Claude was keeping this particular book and her voice to herself while I steered through Iowa's cornfields—she looked like she planned on not saying a word for the next five hundred miles. Her luscious hair rolled in waves over her shoulders, but she was wearing overalls, which I don't like because the hardware reminds me of armor and the bib is just one more layer between me and her breasts. If she had on a sleeveless shirt, I could at least get a sideways peek, but she had the air-conditioner on, and sticking out from under the bib and straps was a sweater as thick as chain mail.

I switched the camper to cruise, took my right hand from the hand controls, and laid it on Claude's shoulder. No response. I slipped my fingers under her hair and gripped the nape of her neck.

"You only want me when I'm angry at you," Claudine said.

"Otherwise I wouldn't want you very often," I teased.

Claudine wrenched away from me, smacking her feet on the floor. "How do you expect me to feel? After you said you'd leave me if you had to, looking me right in my face?"

It took me a minute to catch on. "You mean in that song by Fat Stan?" I asked. "I didn't say that, Claude, I sang it. To a whole bar full of people."

"You were looking right at me! You said, 'That's what I'll do'—you'd leave. And then you kept looking at me and you said it again."

"I sang it," I said.

"There's no difference between singing and saying when you're staring like that."

"Claude, I wasn't looking at you! I couldn't see anyone in the audience last night, it was totally dark! And I would never look at you and sing I'd leave you, even if I was thinking that, which I wasn't."

Claude went back to reading, or pretending to read.

⊙

Five hours later, I was sitting in the Blues Jam Café in Champaign, Illinois, waiting for the evening to wear on to showtime, wondering if my marriage was over as I watched Claudine build three-story towers out of a dozen cream thimbles. Lucy was falling asleep on my lap. With her cute little head nestled in the crook of my arm and her toddler-sized All Stars braced against my wheelchair, we looked like the perfect subject for a human-interest story—one of those pieces that hardly mentions my music and gets placed in the "Style" or "Life" rather than the "Entertainment" section of the paper, next to advice columns and recipes and photos of homeless dogs. It would be great if, just once, a journalist would consider me a musician first, and not focus on my disability. But I'm not holding my breath.

I shifted Lucy and tried again to spot the woman I suspected was a reporter. She had disappeared from the dining room. I tried to see into the bar, but it was too dark. I looked at Claudine again, but she still wasn't looking at me.

The last time she got this mad, over a year ago, I truly had gone too far with a fan. Josie, this old girlfriend of mine, showed up on a night Claude had gone to bed early. During the break after my second set, Josie and I went outside for a stroll behind the bar, and when I spun around to start back, her hands found my fly. I could have stopped her, but I did not. As she knew from our high school days, with a lot of stimulation that one part of my lower body still works.

A few days later Claude found Josie's number on a scrap of paper, and then Claude was the one who left me: walked off in between sets, in the middle of the night, in the middle of Missouri. Took a bus back to Detroit and lived with her mother for three months. We might not have got back together at all if Claude hadn't been pregnant with Lucy.

For the past year and a half, since that one act of adultery, I've been faithful to Claude. Fans have shaken my hands, patted my shoulders, and given me hugs, but none of their lips have touched any part of me again, not counting that one kiss last night.

Claudine set an empty cream thimble on top of the tower she was building.

"I feel like I'm sitting in a black hole," I said.

Claudine narrowed her eyes, picking up another cream thimble. She didn't answer.

"Beam me up, Scotty," I said, gripping my wheel rim with my left hand and squeezing little Lucy with my right.

"Get it out of your system now," Claudine said, "or you're going to look like a fool in front of that reporter."

"So that *was* a reporter I saw! Claudine, I asked you not to."

Claudine balanced yet another cream thimble on the foil lid of another. "When you stop encouraging groupies," she said, "I'll stop calling reporters."

"I don't encourage them," I protested.

"At the very least," she said, "you accommodate them."

"They're my fans, Claude. I can't act like I hate them." Just then I noticed the reporter approaching, appearing out of the bar and walking toward us. I waved at her to cover my alarm. My movement disturbed Lucy, who was balanced at the edge of sleep, and she shouted, "Daddy, stop!" and gave my belly a hard kick. I only felt the vibration, as if she'd kicked me through a wall of pillows, but I snapped at her anyway.

"*You* stop," I said. "I'm not going to play any pigeon music tonight unless you go to sleep right this minute." Lucy hurriedly closed her eyes. "Showtime," I warned Claudine, hoping she would act like everything was fine.

"I don't feel like performing," Claude said.

Ah, crap, I thought, and looked up into the reporter's face. "Have a seat," I said, pulling out a chair, no doubt surprising her with my effortless reach—I'm six three, and my arms are long. "I'm Mason Hilliard," I said, "and these are my loyal-est fans, though not always by choice: Lucille, my daughter, and Claudine, my wife."

The reporter laughed, sounding nervous. Then she introduced herself and said, "It's so nice to meet you . . . and your family." She had pale skin, rusty hair, and big, green eyes. Also a pimple on her chin that she must have recently tried to fix—the spot was red and wounded looking.

A fast-moving waitress stopped at our table. The reporter, whose name I'd already forgotten, didn't want anything. "And how are you folks doing?" the waitress asked.

I hate it when they ask that when things are going badly. "Fine," I said. "We're all set for the moment, I think . . ." I looked at Claudine, but she was still messing around with all her little cream containers. The waitress hurried away, and I turned to the reporter.

She asked me a few basic questions: my age (twenty-eight), Lucille's age (eighteen months), who my influences are. Then I told her about my second CD plus the new stuff I'm working on—a jazzier kind of blues that's both ethereal and down to earth, etcetera, etcetera. I paused, and as I watched the reporter scrawling in her notebook, I wondered how many facts would end up slightly altered or completely wrong. A few years back, a reporter put me down as a high school dropout, when the truth is I graduated with honors, though a year late; and a couple months ago, another one wrote me up as an amputee, though I'm not missing so much as a toe. Both of those mistakes had come out of interviews that had gone very well. I'd answered the questions articulately, I'd thought, and added what I wanted to say, and Claudine had been at her best—witty and cheerful and charming.

"So, we're near the end of our summer tour," I volunteered, smoothing Lucy's hair. I could feel by her weight that she'd fallen fast asleep. I added pigeon music to my plans for the evening.

"And what's next on your agenda?" the reporter asked.

"Our fall and winter tour," I said. "We've got one more week of summer, then we'll head right into fall and winter."

"It was his idea to divide things up into seasons," Claude said. "Gives him an illusion of change or order or something." I'd been hoping that Claude would keep quiet. "But fall and winter are really no different than summer or spring. There are more festivals in the summer, and at any time of year we add and drop a handful of bars, but basically we just keep circling."

I moved my water glass and coffee cup aside, then lifted my jacket from the back of my wheelchair and spread it out on the table. "There," I said. "How's that for a little bed?"

With her long lashes shutting me out, Claudine pushed up from her chair and gathered Lucille from me. As soon as Claudine had started to rise, I'd changed my mind about giving up Lucy. I'd felt a pureness flowing from her body, giving me strength. As Claudine eased her from my arms, Lucy sighed and clung to my chest. Claudine continued to gather her up, breaking Lucille's hold, and my little girl murmured, "Daddy," and tried to clutch me in her sleep. I wanted so badly to take her back. Instead I turned my attention to the reporter, who was observing my shoulders, which people tend to stare at, surprised by how broad and muscular they are—I use my arms more than most people do, and I also work out. I lifted my chin and tried to smile, to let the reporter know I was ready for another question.

"This might sound like a dumb question," she said. "But I was wondering... does your ... *handicap* ... interfere with your performance in any way?"

I laced my fingers together with exaggerated gracefulness and placed my hands before me on the table. "No," I said, "not at all. In fact, you could say that my disability has improved my ability to perform."

"You could *say* it," Claudine said.

"Not across the board," I continued, as if Claude hadn't spoken. "For instance, I only have control of my body from my T12 vertebra up. So, if I were playing a piano, I might try to reach too far and fall off the bench." I smiled a little so the reporter would know I was trying to be funny.

"He's not very good at what he calls 'lunging,'" Claudine said matter-of-factly, "on a piano bench or elsewhere."

I jerked in surprise and stared at my wife, though I'd just told myself that the best thing to do was ignore her. I knew she'd uttered such a slur against my manhood thinking only I would catch her meaning. Which didn't mean I was going to let it go. "But I have perfect control of my hands and my mouth," I said to the reporter. "An able-bodied man can't hold a candle. Because of my improved abilities, certain other abilities aren't missed."

"Still," Claudine said, "I can't help wondering how he performed before he fell out of that tree."

The reporter leaned closer. "Falling out of a tree," she said, her green eyes glittering, "Is that how you—"

"Injured my spinal cord? Yes," I said. "But it looks better in print if you simply say that I sustained my injury in a climbing accident."

"He wasn't climbing," Claudine said. "He was standing on a tree branch, high on marijuana, and he tried to *fly*, and he landed on his *head*."

I took hold of the table edge without realizing I was going to, and without any idea of what I planned to do next. I felt stupid sitting there gripping a table edge as if I was thinking of pushing the table over. Finally I said, "I think I'll go get ready for my show."

Claudine turned away with a little I-don't-care flip of her head that made my heart ache. I glanced down at my left wheel and then at my right one to see if I had room to maneuver, then pushed the empty chair of the table behind me out of my way. The reporter rose from her chair and said, "Excuse me, but could I ask . . ."

I manipulated my wheelchair to face her, and she stopped speaking. Up until that moment, the reporter had seen only my muscled arms and chest and my pleasant, even good-looking face. She looked down at my atrophied legs as if she'd stumbled upon the remains of a corpse. I knew that the fear and distaste glittering in her green eyes was instinctive, that it was impersonal, but I hated her for it anyway. *My fingertips,* I thought, *are more adept than your whole body.* "You had another question?" I said.

The reporter fixed her gaze on my left shoulder and smiled crookedly. "I was going to ask," she said, "if your being in a wheelchair has any relationship to the fact that you play the blues."

I glanced from the reporter's pasted-on smile to Claudine's unfocused eyes, which were still not meeting mine, even though we'd shot each other looks over this question every other time it was asked. "Actually, no," I replied evenly. We'd learned to leave it at that. But this time I added, "My wife provides me with all the inspiration and motivation I need." Claudine glanced at me with hurt, angry surprise and looked away. I tried to ignore the tightness in my throat and chest. "If you want to know the truth," I said to the reporter, "I got into the blues when I was thirteen, which was years before I met Claudine, and also before I fell out of that tree." I stuck out my hand. "Nice to have met you. And sorry we screwed up the interview."

The reporter protested unintelligibly. She looked embarrassed, and as if she couldn't wait to get away. I doubted she'd stay to hear even my first set, and so she'd keep her distorted opinion of me.

I maneuvered my chair through the crowded dining room, finally making it to the front door and out. There I popped a wheelie and, balancing on my rear wheels, I lowered myself down the stairs one step at a time, though there was no handrail to grab if I lost control. *Hell*, I thought, feeling a smile crack my face, *I've fallen farther than this.*

I wheeled up and down the length of the block. I took some deep breaths. The tightness in my lungs and throat began to ease.

What really happened is way different than what Claudine told that reporter. Claude wasn't even there—she didn't know me then. And although several people saw me fall, I'm the only one who really knows what it was like—from when I started up the tree to when I hit the ground and everything in between.

What happened was this:

I'd smoked some weed with my brother and two of his friends and two girls on the drive out to Kent Lake. When we got there they lit another bowl, and I started up the scarred knobs of a tall pine. "Mace, you monkey, bring your butt back down here," my brother called. He probably thought I was too doped to climb. "No crazy stuff this time," he shouted up after me. I didn't look down at him or answer.

At first I climbed carelessly, without a plan, simply enjoying the feel of moving upward. But soon heaviness slid into my arms and legs, and though I wasn't cold, I began to shake—the truth is, I'm afraid of heights. My hands closed around branches as if trying to fuse with them. I felt my sweat growing cool, though the day was mild and there was hardly any breeze. I continued to climb, trying to ignore what was happening to me, but finally, as I always did, I stopped and just stood there gripping the tree, feeling the rough bark against the skin of my palms. "This is silly," I said to myself. "I'm scared. What am I trying to prove?" But then I told myself, *Go on, just a little higher.* And I kept going up—hand over hand, foot after foot—until soon my thoughts had drifted, and both my high and my fear had left me, as I'd known they would.

I was wearing an old sweat suit and my red low-tops— perfect climbing clothes, perfect clothes for jumping. Feeling light and keen and extremely alive, I climbed higher with incredible confidence, but also with incredible care. I was a long way from the ground. When the trunk thinned so that I could span it with my hands, I stopped and looked down at my brother and his friends and the girls. They looked very far away. I could see they'd stopped passing the pipe. They were all watching me, faces lifted and motionless.

I looked across to the nearest tree, another pine. It had very few lower branches, and so its higher branches were easy to see from the ground. I'd jumped to that tree before. That day I chose a different branch. I looked at it for a long time, studying its angle, its roundness and thickness, its flaky, brownish-gray bark. And then I leapt.

It feels like this:

First a singing, close-to-screaming joy and fear in my throat and gut and every bit of my body. An indescribable moment of *touching nothing.* Then the relief of feeling rough bark gripped by my hands, solid wood underneath. Only this time the wood wasn't solid, and the branch I grasped held at first but then snapped cleanly with my weight, and as my feet continued their upward swing, I dove downward, head first.

I watched tree limbs passing me as if they were falling and I was holding still, and then the branches seemed to slow, and I did, too—almost to a stop, it seemed. I floated downward, trees upside down all around me. Something punched my shoulder, hard—a branch—but it didn't hurt. A wonderful, dreamy spinning turned slowly in my chest and throat and head. I felt more awake and alive than I'd ever felt. I wasn't afraid. I couldn't stop what was happening, and I didn't want to.

Afterwards, I was bitter for months, a seemingly endless amount of time because until I stopped being bitter, I didn't know if I ever would. There was a span of days when I really lost it—I just cried and stayed in bed. But I didn't want to die. So I had to get up. And I went back to school, I began playing harmonica again, and my life became worth it again. And the fall—well, the fall became amazing again, as it was when it was happening.

I told all this once to a reporter I'd gone to high school with, and she did a pretty good job of getting it down. But her editor said that the story was too frightening for his family magazine. He said he could run a story about my recovery, but not about my fall. "The description after the moment of impact is too terrible," the editor said, "and I don't see any way around it. You can't write about the fall without saying how it ends. You can't leave the guy up in the air."

⊙

I sprinted the length of the block once more, reaching far back on my push rims and *thrusting* forward, flying past shop fronts and parked cars. Then, without pausing a beat, I stroked around to the alley and sprinted down its length, passing our camper, which was giving off an amber glow—we'd left a light on, as usual, to find our way back in the dark. After slaloming around some trash cans, I popped a wheelie up the single step of the Blues Jam's rear entrance and maneuvered through the kitchen, saying, "How's it going?" to the cook, who answered, "Not too bad." Then I glided out into the dining room. Claudine and Lucy were gone. I wanted to race out of the café and see if I could find them—in our camper, packing a bag for the road, or maybe Claudine was already hurrying down the street with Lucy in her arms. But even if I caught up with them, I knew I couldn't prevent my hard-headed wife from leaving, if that's what she wanted to do.

Usually, even if Lucy is asleep, Claudine waits to put her down until after my first set, so I sat at our table hoping they'd only gone to the washroom and would come right back. But it was a bad sign that Claude had taken all of their stuff— Claudine's sweater, Lucy's little hoodie and her binky and stuffed dog.

I met Claude on a night like this one, four years ago, at the Raven Lounge in Detroit. I was by myself and kind of down, but I knew I'd feel better once I picked up a harp and started blowing. That's the best thing about the blues: they take you through your pain and bring you back to joy—if not completely, then at least part of the way.

I noticed Claude the moment she walked into the Raven. I was so blown away by her beauty. Her hair was bouncing up around her shoulders, and she was tall and all curves—even her eyelashes were curvy. And her eyes looked right at me, from head to toe, taking me all the way in. She came to my show the next night, stayed till the end, helped me pack up, and spent the night in my van. Two weeks later, she quit her job and joined me on the road. After our first year together, we got married and traded my van for a camper, and after Lucille was born, we made some adjustments to my schedule. But lately Claude's been talking about wanting to settle down in one place, and I don't blame her. I can't make a living, though, staying in a single city or town, and I doubt she'll trust me, now that I screwed around with Josie, to travel from gig to gig on my own.

I sat at our empty table—the coffee mugs and water glasses and cream containers had been cleared away—hoping and waiting for Claude and Lucy to return. Ten minutes later, with no sign of them, I started toward the plywood ramp Claude had set against the stage before we ordered dinner.

The ramp lay at a steep angle, with not enough floor area free of tables on which I could get a rolling start, so I approached a man who looked sober and as if he knew how to use his body and told him what I wanted. The man was glad to be of help. He pushed me up the ramp super cautiously, as if he was afraid I might break. I wanted to say, *C'mon, man, I already did that, right?* But I thanked the guy and turned my attention to my equipment.

Before dinner I had set up and tested my mixing board and amplifier and speakers. I'd leaned my guitars against the back of the stage with their necks up so I could reach them easily, and I'd laid my harmonicas on the far edge of the board all in a row, in the order I wanted. Claudine usually does these things for me, but tonight I'd offered to do it myself, and she didn't object. I imagined her striding down the street, lugging Lucy on her hip. But most likely they had only gone out to our camper, and I'd find them sleeping there when I was done for the night. I considered going out to check on them before starting my show, but I had three sets to get through, and if they were gone, I didn't want to know that yet.

Thinking I'd start off with an easy instrumental to get my lungs working and put off using my voice, which I'm always afraid will fail me when I'm not feeling so great, I plugged in my Lee Oskar D, whipped the cord over my shoulder, and blew a riff softly, adjusted the mix and tried again, then a few more times. Finally, I wheeled up close to the voice mike. "Well," I said, "it's blues time."

A dozen faces turned toward me. The room was nearly full, half of the crowd talking with each other or playing with their phones or drinks and ignoring me completely, the other half glancing at me with interest or at least a willingness to get interested.

"Yes, it's blues time," I said again. "It's showtime. I'm Mason Hilliard, and this is a tune written by a friend of mine named Stanley Clarence. The tune's called 'Violet,' and it goes like this."

I played, listening to myself carefully at first, reaching out to the board and adjusting the mix until it sounded exactly right, then letting my gaze roam over the crowd, from the close tables to the booths near the walls and the doorway to the bar. I recognized, or thought I did, two, maybe three faces, though not to call by name. My best local friend was out of town, and another friend wouldn't be coming till sometime after ten, and maybe not at all—he hadn't known if he could get away. Thinking of the woman who had thrown herself at me last night and all the trouble that had caused, thinking that I might have to get through three sets without friends and the rest of my life without Claudine, I finished "Violet" with more speed and heat than Fat Stan intended when he wrote it. The crowd clapped with spirit, and a booth full of men shouted and hooted appreciatively, keeping it up after I'd brought my lips close to the mike again, making me wait for them a little too long. I hoped their enthusiasm wouldn't turn into a roaring appreciation of their own drunkenness. I don't like an audience to listen to me as closely as to a symphony, but I like it even less when they don't connect with me at all.

While I waited for the rowdies to settle down, I searched the crowd for Claudine. She was nowhere in the room, but my gaze found the reporter standing at the back wall. It looked like she was paying attention and appreciating my show. Maybe she'd write a decent story after all.

I decided to do a song especially for Claudine. Switching harps, I turned up the sound as loud as I dared and started in on one of Claude's favorites, a 1930s blues classic called "Further on Down the Road." And so that Claude, if she could hear me from our camper, would know who I was singing to, no mistake, I added some words of my own: "*Claude, come with me—Claude, I'm hoping—Claudine, can you hear me prayin'?*"

I sang the refrain twice, drawing it out. Then I opened my eyes, willing Claudine to materialize back at our table. No such luck. Probably she was asleep, or else reading her book. I didn't think she would leave me tonight. But it was starting to sink in that, sooner or later, I'd be going further down the road without her. I looked away from the empty chair where she'd sat tonight and saw this picture in my mind: it's daytime, and she's not walking away but on a train, our little Lucy sitting beside her. Claude's hair is pulled back. Lucy's wearing a dress and looks older—a little girl, not a toddler. They're both staring ahead, with faraway looks in their eyes. I'm nowhere near the train; I'm completely out of the picture. They can't see me or hear me, and even if they could, Claude is done with listening to me.

I picked up my Gibson, mounted a brand-new Japanese harp on its stand, and played "Love in Vain." At the end of the song, I blew a long improvisational riff. That brought whistles, shouts of appreciation, and a burst of applause. Pain stirred in my chest, then thrust outward and disappeared. My chest still hurt, but with a smoother, slighter ache.

I decided to do another instrumental, one of my own, a fast, wild little tune with a slow feeling buried inside all the motion. "This one's called 'Free Fall,'" I said after the crowd had gathered in closer. *This will gather you in further*, I thought, and I breathed everything I had into it.

It's a tune that took me years to get right. It's the tune of my fall, but of more than I could take in while it was happening:

Besides the trees and the whirling, besides the utter sweetness of falling, of floating, almost still, it takes in the sky at my feet, and the gravity of the earth pulling me down, and the people watching me, with fear and with love.

They can't stop what is happening—they're unable to save me.

I'm all alone—I'm set apart.

I'm speeding toward them and getting closer.

But I'll never reach them, not completely. And yet I'm aiming straight for their hearts.

Losing
It

Hovering near an oak tree, Thomas peers down at the street—since his death, his vision has rivaled Superman's, yet he can't make sense right now of what he's seeing. Sod has been laid over the asphalt: for the length of a block and from curb to curb. At the center of the sod, burning on top of it, is a strip of coals the size of a bowling lane.

"Do you know what you're about to witness?" Gerald asks, hovering beside Thomas.

"A huge marshmallow roast—no, I mean a religious ritual?" Thomas guesses, treading air by scissoring his feet. He hasn't been dead as long as Gerald has; Gerald hovers without effort.

"The practitioners consider it a form of therapy," Gerald answers. He points beyond the burning coals to a nearby building. "The one I want you to watch is a man named Jeremy Byrd. He's a nurse who has a terrible problem with his temper. Look—there's your man now: the big guy with the bronze curls."

"He looks like a Greek god," Thomas says, blurting, as usual, the first thing that pops into his head.

"Well, he's not," Gerald answers. "He's just a man, and, other than his looks, his only godlike attribute is his talent for massage. Jeremy's huge hands can cover a whole small back at once; they can enclose a medium thigh. And reach down, so I'm told, through flesh, fat, and bone to the tight places within the soul. But those same big hands, teamed up with his temper? Well, we'll get to that later."

A hundred men and women, Jeremy among them, walk down the stairs of a darkened health club and fan out on the expanse of sod. "What an odd way to play strip poker," Thomas says, looking the people over. Most seem dressed for a day at the office, except that everyone has stripped from the knees down: those wearing pants have rolled them up, and all socks, hose, and shoes have been discarded.

As if at a signal, a thousand toes wiggle in the grass, and a murmur rises from the group like a cloud: "Ahhh, oooohhh, mmmm."

"What planet is this?" Thomas asks. He's making a joke; he'd seen at once that these were North Americans, the sort of people he'd known all his life.

"It's Earth," Gerald answers, missing the humor.

Thomas keeps his sigh to himself, but he can't help wondering why grim bureaucrats always get to be in charge.

"We're in Ann Arbor, Michigan," Gerald continues, keeping his gaze on the crowd.

Ann Arbor! Thomas thinks fondly; during one of his lives,

he drove there often to escape Detroit. Thomas remembers playing Frisbee in a park, smoking weed on the street, watching girls walking around without bras. Ann Arbor lay only fifty miles west of Detroit, but it seemed like a world away.

"Watch Jeremy now," Gerald says. "See that folded-up scrap of paper in his hand? Read it."

Thomas squints. "It says, *I'm afraid of losing it.* Of losing what?"

Gerald holds up a finger for silence. "Just watch."

Jeremy stretches out his arm and tosses the paper onto the coals; all around him other people toss their own folded scraps of paper. "They're burning their fears," Gerald explains.

Thomas reads the others' fears to himself: *I'm afraid of dying. I'm afraid of flying. I'm afraid of the IRS. I'm afraid of my wife finding out. I'm afraid of falling from bridges. I'm afraid of falling in love.* The scraps of paper burn and disintegrate into the coals. "In a few minutes," Gerald says, "they'll conquer their fear of walking on fire. By doing so, they hope to gain the confidence to master their other fears."

A fire-walk leader throws a stick onto the coal bed. The wood smokes, then jumps with flame. "Fire's too hot yet," Gerald says. "Their feet would burn."

"Is that why I'm here?" Thomas asks. "To keep Jeremy's feet from burning?"

"Sweat and faith will take care of his feet," Gerald says. "You're here to help him with what he wrote on the paper."

"'I'm afraid of losing it'?" Thomas asks.

"Yes," Gerald answers. "Jeremy has a long history of losing it. Let me show you what I mean."

The sound comes in before the picture does: a crash like

glass exploding followed by a tinkling like crazed wind chimes. Then Thomas sees ceramic shards scattered at the edge of a basement floor. Across the room, a teenaged Jeremy looms over an electric kiln. Jeremy reaches into the kiln and lifts out what looks like an ashtray or a flat bowl. He turns the object in his hands, studying it as if it is something he has found rather than made. Then he draws back his arm and hurls the failed piece at the far wall. Reaching into the kiln again, he lifts out what looks like a *bigger* ashtray, or perhaps a dish for a large dog. Again, Jeremy draws back his arm and lets the piece fly.

The tinkling subsides and the scene disappears, replaced by an image of a slightly older Jeremy behind the wheel of a rusting Toyota. A dark-haired girl sits beside him. The girl's lips are moving, but no words are coming out. "We've lost the sound," Gerald says. "I'll have to narrate. Okay, here's Jeremy driving with his girlfriend. 'Turn left,' she says, so Jeremy starts turning left." The car floats in slow motion. Gerald's voice quickens like a sportscaster's: "He's in the middle of the inter-section, he's starting his leftward curve, he's halfway through the turn . . . 'No, I mean turn right!' his girlfriend says." Gerald falls silent. Jeremy's fist flies up from the stick shift. A spider web blooms across the windshield.

The scene shifts again. "Here you see Jeremy a few years older but no wiser, attacking the foundation of his house with a screwdriver. You see, he's trying to replace his Volvo's alter-nator, but every time he tries to unscrew it, he gets shocked."

"Why doesn't he just disconnect the battery?" Thomas asks.

Gerald shrugs. The setting changes to indoors, a home office, Jeremy pounding on the lid of a printer.

"He seems to have a problem with modern technology," Thomas says. "Couldn't we move him to another century?"

Gerald shakes his head. "He's where he belongs."

"What if we count him as one of the lost?" Thomas asks, not sure if he's joking, or even what being one of the lost means.

"That's what you're here to prevent," Gerald answers, shifting his gaze to a fire-walk leader who is dropping another stick onto the coal bed. The stick smokes slowly, then creeps with flame. "Couple more minutes," Gerald says. "I've got business elsewhere. Any questions before I go?"

"Yeah," Thomas says. "What am I supposed to do with this guy?"

"Watch over him," Gerald answers. "You're his guardian."

"For how long?"

"As long as he needs you." Gerald begins to dissolve into the air.

"But what if I don't want to?" Thomas asks.

Gerald smiles, his mind already gone, his soul fading.

"I really don't think I want to!" Thomas says, but Gerald has disappeared.

"I want pie in the sky," Thomas says, not sure whether he is speaking to Gerald or to himself. "That's what I was looking forward to, not this—this is too much like life! This is work! This is *not* how I want to spend my death!"

With enviable swiftness and precision, Gerald flies right in Thomas's face. "There's no pie up here. No coffee, either. And you better see that Jeremy doesn't lose it, or you're going to lose it." Quick as a whirlwind, Gerald is gone.

"Lose what?" Thomas says softly. "What are you going to do? Break my thumbs? Shoot my kneecaps?" He looks down at his insubstantial body and laughs. But his laughter is brittle and false, and he feels, somewhere near the center of his soul, a twisting in his cloudy heart.

⊙

Jeremy makes it across the coals: mouth popped wide, huge hands flapping at his sides, but without injury to his size 14 feet. In the following weeks, his days are filled with nothing but good behavior—Jeremy doesn't lose it once. But then, on a morning almost like any other, after searching for his wallet for fifteen minutes without success, Jeremy bellows, "I hate this! Life is full of crap!" He whips his keys down at the floor. The keys clunk as they nail the carpet. Then silence and stillness resume. The keys lie transfixed, as if under a spell, spread out like a pinwheel on their ring.

Jeremy bends over the keys. Then he picks them up. The carpet is unmarred. Nothing is broken. No one has seen him or heard him—Jeremy's wife is at work. Jeremy sighs with relief and slips the keys into his pocket.

That was good! Thomas says. No harm done, and you let off some steam.

A week later, Jeremy comes home from buying groceries to find his wife's cat preparing to retch: the runty animal is dry-heaving with its mouth aimed at the kitchen rug. Quick! Snatch her up! Thomas says. Jeremy sets down the grocery bags and strides lightly toward the cat, calling her urgently yet gently, his arms outstretched in a reassuring manner.

The cat whips her face toward Jeremy, freezes with a look of panic, and streaks into the living room. Thomas laughs. Jeremy curses and hurries after the cat, forcing his big feet to tread lightly, without threat. Thomas follows Jeremy, ready to offer more advice, but, rounding the corner of the L-shaped room, he sees the cat vomiting on the plush carpeting. Oh, sick! Thomas thinks, turning away, hoping his weak stomach hasn't followed him into death. To be safe, he keeps his back to the room, humming to himself while Jeremy shouts.

"Little Darling! Come here! Stay there!" Jeremy tries to reach the cat, but just as he touches the outer wisps of her fur, she slips from his big hands and runs; stopping under the coffee table, she resumes her rhythmic spasming. Jeremy waits for the cat to finish. Then he snatches her up. "You stupid, stupid cat," he says. "I only wanted to put you outside before you ruined the damned rug!"

Afraid she might not be done vomiting, Jeremy holds Little Darling at arm's length with both hands and carries her to the door leading to the stoop. There he clamps her under his left arm like a football so that he can unfasten the bolt with his free hand; but as he fumbles with the lock, the cat squirms to face his chest and clings, piercing shirt and flesh as if they are tree bark. By the time Jeremy has managed to get the first door open, the cat is almost out of his grasp, writhing and clawing backward up his left shirtsleeve and arm. Jeremy unlatches the second door; propping it open with one big foot, he takes the cat firmly in both his hands. He has an excellent grip on the cat now, but he doesn't want to hold her another second. He also doesn't want to let her go. As if on its own, his right thumb slides over the cat's windpipe.

Thinking he had better put a stop to things, Thomas flutters into the kitchen. But when he sees the tiny cat gripped by Jeremy's huge hands, he says something opposite to what he had intended: You could wring that cat's neck like a chicken.

Jeremy freezes like a statue, like a still-frame from a strangler flick. Then, all at once, he wilts, tension draining from his big body and his face. He holds his arms out limply and drops the cat. She lands, without grace but lightly, on her feet.

Jeremy drags himself back to the living room, collapses onto the couch, and begins moaning silently, as if from the depths of his soul.

Oh, stop it, Thomas says.

Despite such directness, Jeremy thinks he is talking to himself. He's been talking to himself a lot lately, he's noticed— ever since he went on that fire walk.

So you almost killed your wife's cat, so what? Thomas says. Didn't you ever almost kill a cat when you were a boy?

No, Jeremy admits.

Then consider yourself a late bloomer, Thomas snaps. He feels like flying off and never coming back; he wishes he were the guardian angel of someone else. Somebody more exciting, or at least more exciting to look at—every day on the street Thomas sees women he'd rather follow. But, even though he doesn't like to admit it, as sorry a human life as Jeremy seems to lead, Thomas is jealous of it. Yesterday at the hospital, when one of the female nurses laid her arm across Jeremy's back and whispered something and Jeremy laughed, Thomas was sick with envy. He wanted a life, any life at all. If he had one, he wouldn't waste one minute of it chasing after a vomiting cat, much less moaning about it afterward.

But Jeremy can't seem to get off the subject. At least I didn't hurt Little Darling, he thinks.

That's right, Thomas says, trying to wrap things up.

I almost threw her, Jeremy thinks, and I considered strangling her, but I didn't—I stopped myself in time. Maybe yelling is okay.

Of course it is, Thomas says. You're not a saint.

But Jeremy is not consoled. He tightens his half-curled hands until they become enormous fists. What am I going to do with myself? he asks.

You could take up boxing, Thomas suggests. It's not too late for a professional career.

I already have a career, Jeremy answers.

Or you could get a job as an enforcer. It wouldn't have to be a career, it could be a hobby.

Jeremy shakes his head. That's not what these hands are for.

Oh, yeah? Thomas says, miffed at being rebuffed. Then what are those muscled, massive hunks of flesh you call hands for?

For massaging my patients, Jeremy says. He opens his hands and wiggles his fingers, his face reflective. For riding my bike.

For picking flowers, Thomas says. For scratching your crotch.

Jeremy smiles, amusement softening his troubled features. For touching my wife, he says. For handling everything gently. He gets up from the couch and goes out to the kitchen and starts unpacking the groceries: a bunch of kale, a tub of tofu, several boxes of herbal tea.

How come you never buy any coffee? Thomas says. You know you like it. Strong. Black. With bacon and fried eggs.

Jeremy unbags a package of rice crackers and a carton of frozen yogurt.

And what about pie? Thomas says. A piece of pie every now and then isn't going to kill you.

Jeremy opens the freezer door and peers into the frosty white space.

I'm warning you, Thomas says. You better start eating pie now, while you've got the chance, because there isn't any after you die.

⊙

A week later, Jeremy rides off on his motorcycle to buy a special lunch for his sick wife. He is on his way home, riding through town with the boxed lunch strapped to his bike, when a Subaru pulls out of a parking lot and turns directly behind him. Thomas is flying above. Uh-oh, he says. That woman doesn't see you, and she's way too close.

Jeremy checks his mirrors. The woman in the Subaru is right on his tail. Barely tall enough to see over the steering wheel, she's looking out the driver's window and waving to someone on the sidewalk. Jeremy is riding at twenty miles per hour. He pushes the bike up to twenty-five. He can't go much faster because there's a red light at the next corner.

The woman driving the Subaru also increases her speed. She is still waving good-bye, turned halfway around in her seat. She hasn't even glanced at the street ahead of her.

Thomas shouts at the woman, but she doesn't hear him—she's not paying attention to anything! Steady, he says to Jeremy. Oh, no—hold on tight! The Subaru taps the back of Jeremy's bike, and the bike leaps into the air. Keep her steady!

Thomas shouts, and Jeremy does; he keeps the bike pointing straight ahead.

The bike lands on its tires and continues to roll, but as it lands it compresses, bottoming out on its springs, and at that moment the Subaru taps the back of the bike again and slides up onto the seat, tilting the bike backward so that it's doing a wheelie.

The bike and the Subaru are locked like mismatched mating dogs, the bike still in wheelie position, the car's bumper on the back of the bike seat and its front wheels spinning in air—the horror-struck woman has her foot on what she thinks is the brake, and she's holding the pedal to the floor.

The Subaru's front wheels spin in the tractionless air, and the car bumper creeps forward over the upward-slanting bike seat, slowly pushing Jeremy forward. Steady! Thomas shouts. Keep holding her steady! And Jeremy does. But the car continues to inch forward, digging into Jeremy's back, until the bike levels out, its front wheel finally coming back down onto the pavement, and Jeremy is squeezed between the car and his bike, his balls pressing the bike's gas tank.

You can't stay with it any longer! Thomas screams. Get out of there—lean back now!

Jeremy leans back against the hood, but as he lifts his legs over the handlebars, the woman slams on the brake, and Jeremy is launched, feet first, ten feet into the air. The car closes halfway over the fallen bike and finally stops. Jeremy comes down a few yards up the street. He lands hard, but on his feet; he doesn't fall—he doesn't even stutter-step. His size 14 shoes grip the pavement, and his extra-large hands, spread at his sides, give him the balance of wings.

Jeremy stares out through the visor of his helmet without moving from where he has landed. He turns his head toward a man on the sidewalk who has stopped walking his dog. Jeremy and the man stare at each other open-mouthed, the man slowly shaking his head. Thomas forgets to flutter his feet and almost falls out of the sky. He recovers himself and follows Jeremy as Jeremy stalks back toward the Subaru.

The tiny woman is still sitting in the driver's seat, her window rolled up though the day is warm. "Fuck," Jeremy says, looking down at his bike protruding from under the Subaru. The bike is mangled beyond repair. It's almost cut in half. "Fuck!" Jeremy says again, louder, looking around without focusing.

Then he begins to jump around. As soon as he comes down, he jumps up again, leaping up and down and sideways, too, around to the front of the car where his bike lies, then back to the driver's window. "You could have killed me!" he shouts. "You almost did! And look what you did to my bike! Just look at it! It's trash!"

Stopping to gaze in amazement at the crumpled components of his bike, Jeremy notices the smashed box containing what's left of his wife's lunch. "And my wife's lunch!" he croaks, his voice breaking. "You ruined my wife's lunch!" He stops at the driver's window and glares in at the glass-shielded woman; she gazes back at him with the dulled, blank look of utter fear.

Jeremy takes his helmet off and grips it in his right hand by the chin strap.

Whoa! Thomas warns. You don't want to do that!

Jeremy doesn't seem to hear. He eyes the windshield, the helmet swaying in his grasp.

Jeremy! Thomas shouts. Remember what you said? What you said your hands are for?

Jeremy's grip on the helmet loosens. He chucks it behind him and looks up at about twenty people staring at him from the curb.

Thomas feels the air stir beside him. "Well," Gerald says, "that's it, I guess."

"What do you mean?" Thomas asks.

"He's done for," Gerald says. "He really lost it good."

"What are you talking about?" Thomas says. "He was going to break the windshield, but he stopped himself! Didn't you see him right now chuck his helmet into the street?"

"I saw him leaping all over the street like a giant frog gone berserk," Gerald says, "screaming and swearing, nearly scaring that little woman to death."

"Well, what about what she nearly did to him?" Thomas counters. "If he hadn't kept his wits, he'd look like his bike now! He'd look like his wife's lunch! Besides, I told him yelling was okay."

"I know you did."

"You're not going to hold that against him, are you?" Thomas asks. "You're not going to punish him, are you, after that miraculous escape?"

"He set his own terms," Gerald says. "He dug his own grave."

"He said he was afraid of losing it, he didn't promise that he wouldn't!" Thomas protests. "Besides, did you see how he landed? He landed on his feet! The man flew like a bird— he flew like a fucking angel! And he landed on his feet! We should give him a medal!"

"Please lower your voice," Gerald says. "And stop swearing."

"Congratulations, Jeremy!" Thomas shouts. "I'm damned proud of you! You did a hell of a job!"

"One more outburst and you're in as much trouble as Jeremy. Already things don't look too good for you."

"I don't believe this!" Thomas says. "He might as well have smashed the windshield!"

Jeremy picks up the helmet.

"Stop him or you're in deep," Gerald says.

Thomas laughs. "In deep? I'm already in deep—I'm dead!"

Gerald grabs Thomas by his quivering heart.

Jeremy! Thomas shouts. Jeremy!

Jeremy glances around him. He looks at the crowd of people on the curb, then at the windows of the buildings lining the street, then straight up, at the sky. Squinting against the sunlight, he hurls the helmet high with all his might. The helmet speeds toward Gerald and Thomas like a comet. It strikes Gerald in the pit of his hollow chest. Gerald lets out a cry like the honk of a goose and disappears into the air.

A siren wails. A police car arrives. Jeremy is standing in the middle of the street. "That woman ran into me—she almost killed me!" he tells the older of the two policemen. "And then I heard a ghost calling my name. I threw my helmet at him to scare him off, but he's still hanging around, I can feel him, I know I can, he's right behind me!"

Thomas edges over an inch and shrinks in on himself.

"Try to calm down," the policeman says. "You've had a near-death experience. Naturally you're upset."

That's right, Thomas agrees.

Jeremy shakes his head as if to rid himself of a waking dream, and bends over what's left of his motorcycle. He grasps a crumpled fender and tugs on it softly, as if he thinks he can lift his bike like a piece of crumpled foil, and it will magically release all of its crimps and folds and be as smooth as when he first saw it in the window of the dealer. As Jeremy fingers the mangled fender, two thoughts reach him at once: I almost died—I have twenty payments left.

Don't worry about losing your bike, Thomas tells him. And "almost" dying doesn't count.

Oh, Jeremy thinks, his failure hitting him all at once, I almost lost it completely. He looks down at his trembling hands. I did lose it—I lost it bad.

You didn't lose a thing, Thomas says. You had a car gnawing your back like a shark, you flew through the air like a dead man, and you ended up alive and without a scratch.

But I almost killed that little woman, Jeremy protests.

So what? Thomas says. That woman deserved to die, driving the way she did. But she got out of it, and so did you. You get another chance.

Jeremy exhales a cloud of stale breath. He scans the street, trying to see beyond the people still staring at him from the curb. Some of the faces are solemn, some are curious, and others are watching him in wonder, as if he's come back from the other side of the veil. Jeremy feels as if he has returned from that border, and as if everything around him—the street with its sprinkling of glass, the heat of the sun on his face, the grit caught up by the warm breeze—is more tangible and visceral than he remembers it being. He squats down and fingers a piece of sharp-edged bright mirror.

Don't be afraid, Thomas says. Walk away from this wreckage. Enjoy your life.

Then Thomas turns away and rises into the sky. He has no idea of where he is going, and he doesn't care—it feels indescribably good simply to move through the air. Yes, to fly! Before he died, he only imagined flying in his dreams.

Jeremy feels suddenly alone. Pressing a knee to the street, he slips the shard of mirror into his pocket and remembers riding his bike fast: zooming north, no destination, leaving all he's ever known behind him. He vows to ride like that again.

But first, he'll buy his wife another lunch. And also something for himself: lemon meringue, or coconut cream. Rising to his feet, Jeremy glances up and down the street, looking for a restaurant, and a bakery.

To the Destroying Angels

I remember watching Darwin gliding back to England on *The Beagle*, fishes swimming beneath the ship as he sailed for home, birds flying overhead and, in the boat's hold, all those dead animals and notes and other evidence that God does not exist.

Well, who am I, then?

Not He, but s~he. I often present as a lateral hermaphrodite: testicle on the right, ovary on the left, small penis or large clitoris—call it what you want—hormones from both gonads coursing through my blood. At times I look human: half man and half woman. If you're wondering whether I'm white or brown, remember that race is *your* invention. And that I take a variety of other forms: from dinosaur to whooping crane, from blade of grass to black-eyed pea.

If you still want to call me god, fine. But if you're going to think of me as God with a capital G, then think Honeybee with a capital H and Elephant with a capital E. And for those of you endlessly waiting for my return, open your eyes and look around! I'm back on your planet almost every day. One of the reasons I return, again and again, is to play another game of basketball, on the streets of Manila and Detroit. I come back to feel that sting of sweat and pleasure, and to call it mine. But that's all that belongs to me: my perceptions and sensations. The rest of you belong to each other and to yourselves. I never made any claim on you, or on those who came before you. Anyone who says differently is lying or deluded.

While I'm at it, I'd like to dispel a few other myths: I've not condoned a single war. I've never caused a hurricane. *Not one* of your religions or governments has earned a place in my regard. Do I seem bitter and angry? Are you wondering why? *It's because* you *are the destroying angels of this Earth*—which, by the way, is among my favorite planets.

The only reason I haven't wiped you off the face of this globe—well, there are two reasons, really. One, because it looks like you're going to do it all by yourselves, and sooner rather than later; and, two, because whenever I look at a human baby, I'm filled with *agape* and awe. If only there were someone other than adult humans to raise these lovely creatures. They are such promising little animals, and yet gradually, you taint them, you turn them into replicas of yourselves. I used to think that atheists were my favorite humans, but really, I like babies best. Babies hungry for the world and drinking it in, through their mouths, eyes, hands, and skin. "Da-da-da," a human baby says, and no, she is not saying "Daddy" or "Papa"—that's just you fathers appropriating a child's first exclamation. She is calling out to me: her true father, her first mother. She is saying, *I'm here, with you—are you here, with me?* She is proclaiming her existence, hoping she's not alone. And she is the reason I put up with the rest of you: why I have never, or at least not yet, given up hope.

Spin

On the weekend of the winter solstice, Murray and I drive across the state to celebrate an early Christmas with my parents. The main event the four of us are looking forward to is a show by James Carter, a native Detroiter and world-renowned sax player. We saw him at the Jazz Fest over Labor Day weekend, we heard his bright, swift notes stream out into the blue summer sky, and we also heard the rocking group that will join him on this night, a Django Reinhardt–inspired quintet called Hot Club of Detroit.

Now it is forty degrees colder, a huge snowstorm hit Detroit yesterday, and the streets have not been plowed. All except the ones most traveled are filled with ridges of slush and snow; higher mounds of snow rise between the sidewalks and the streets. We think we might have trouble parking and then walking to the club, especially since my dad is unsteady on his feet, so I suggest we take a cab. But first my mom calls the club and asks about the parking situation. "Oh, wonderful," she says. "Great." Then she hangs up and announces, "We can drive there—they have valet parking."

We ride down in the elevator of my parents' condo, and I leave my mom and dad and Murray in the lobby and walk out into the garage to retrieve my car. It's a good car for slush and snow—a Subaru with all-wheel drive. The man I bought it from secondhand gave me an extra key and said, "This is the valet key."

I turned it over in my palm.

"It'll start the car, but it won't open the trunk," the man explained. "So when you use a valet service, you can lock your valuables in the trunk."

What valuables? I thought. And I never use valet service. Now, three years later, I can't remember where I've put the key. But the only things in my trunk are a rusty shovel, an old umbrella, and some flattened cardboard I've been meaning to recycle.

As I near the far end of the parking garage, I feel a little nervous, as I often do when walking alone by rows of cars at night. But I remind myself that my parents' garage is surrounded by high walls, has a gatehouse at the entrance, and is watched over, day and night, by security personnel. Upon reaching my car, I unlock it with the remote, get in, and drive up and around to the doors of the lobby, where the pavement has been plowed and the sidewalk shoveled and salted. Murray grips my dad's arm and helps him into the back seat. The seat belts are a little tricky, and what with the darkness and my dad's slow fingers, my parents can't get my dad locked in. "Oh, forget it," my dad says. "It's only a mile from here. You're not going to crash tonight, are you, Annie?"

"I don't think so," I say.

Then we are off down the slushy, snow-rutted streets, with more snow falling and my mom and dad and I arguing about what's the best route to reach the club. Murray looks out at the bright towers of the Renaissance Center and the stone tigers of the new baseball stadium and keeps his opinions about how to get there to himself. But then, he doesn't know Detroit like we do. He grew up an hour east of South Bend, Indiana, where the roads run between fields of beans and corn and where you can still spot Amish buggies, and he's only been a part of my life and my trips to Detroit for the past couple of years.

The tires of cars have sculpted the snow and slush on the city's streets into waves. I drive in the troughs of the waves, the ruts of the slush, and turn left onto Gratiot. When my parents first moved to Detroit, a half century ago, my dad stopped several people to ask them where Gratiot was, using its original French pronunciation: Grah-tee-oh. Finally, the third person he stopped told my dad to spell the street's name.

"Oh," the man responded. "You mean Grass-shit. Grass-shit's right over there."

We turn right onto Brush. I lived two miles north of here for most of my childhood. We turn left onto Adams and pass Grand Circus Park, where as a teenager—most of my lifetime ago—I used to hang out after taking the bus downtown. Next we turn right onto Woodward, Detroit's main street, which I traveled by foot, bike, bus, and car thousands of times. Then we turn left and left again, and finally I pull up as close as I can to Cliff Bell's, stopping behind a car idling right outside the club's door. Cliff Bell's opened a little over a year ago, and my parents came here last Christmas, but Murray and I have never seen the place until now. It's on the left side of a one-way street, so my dad has to get out in the middle of the street rather than by the curb. Not that there is a serviceable curb—it's buried under heaps of snow. But at least there is a shoveled space right in front of the club's entrance.

Murray gets out of the car and strides toward the club to locate the valet. I open my window and call him back. "Murray!" He doesn't seem to hear me. "Murray!" I say again. My dad, who doesn't like to ask for help, has pulled himself out of the back seat and is standing in the two-lane street, tentatively shuffling his feet as he tries to gain a firm footing in the slush. "*Murray!*" I shout. Murray turns around. "Come help my dad!" I call. "Take his arm!"

Murray hurries back toward the car, and I keep my gaze on my dad, hoping he won't fall, until his arm is interlocked with Murray's. My mom, who is almost as sure-footed as I am, is carefully making her way from the car's other side through the waves of slush.

As I continue to watch the three of them, a man appears at my open window, says something about parking my car, and holds out his hand for my keys. I set the keys in his open palm. He opens my door, and I gingerly step out into the slushy street.

The valet is a head taller than me, about Murray's height. His brown skin is a shade lighter than his insulated coat, and he has a scruffy look about him, like the parking attendants who work the downtown lots. A skinny cigar, burned halfway down and no longer lit, sticks out from his chapped lips. He could be my age—just over fifty—or ten or fifteen years younger, smoking, cold weather, and other rough elements having taken their toll. I glance past the valet to my father and am relieved to see that he has made it onto the cleared side-walk. My mom also is standing where the pavement is cleared.

"It's twenty dollars," the valet says.

I return my gaze to his face. Freckles or age spots speckle the skin below his eyes. If I were here with only Murray, I would say, *Forget it, I'll park it myself.* But I don't want to create a stir while out with my folks, especially since they are treating us to the rest of the evening, so I take out my wallet, pull out a twenty, and give it to the man. I've looked past him again to Murray, who is heading toward us, when the valet says, "You need to come with me."

I glance around and then down at the man—while I was looking away, he slipped behind the wheel of my car. "Why?" I ask.

"So I can give you the keys."

I frown down at him, squinting. What the hell does he mean?

Murray looms beside me.

"She needs to come with me," the valet insists.

"*Why?*" I ask again, still confused and starting to get irritated.

"So I can show you where I park and give you the keys."

What lousy valet service! Not really valet service—just crappy parking service. And how stupid does he think I am? No woman in her right mind would drive off into the night with some man she doesn't know, not even in the little town I live in, let alone in Detroit.

"She needs to come with me," the valet insists, gripping the steering wheel and looking out through the windshield, impatient to get going.

Still scowling, I turn to Murray and say, "*I'm* not going with him—*you* go with him."

"Okay," Murray says, obliging as always, and he walks around to the passenger door and gets in. I turn my back on them and navigate my way through the ridges of slush toward the club, wondering if I should complain to the management about the club's parking arrangements and the valet's attitude. But when I step inside the door, the employee stationed there—a pasty young white man wearing a black suit and round black hat with a narrow brim that makes me think of the Amish—is attending to other patrons. I look around, see where my parents are seated, and start toward them, still a little angry. As I pass the front window, I hear a horn blare and look out at the street and see my car. Is that my horn? I sometimes toot or honk but never lean on it, so I'm not sure what sound leaning on it would make. The valet's cigar is still between his lips, and he looks angry. Beyond him, I can just barely make out Murray sitting in the shotgun seat. The valet cuts sharply around the car in front of him, and then they are gone from the window's frame.

◉

My parents are sitting at a table up near the front of the room, which is still three-quarters empty. James Carter always draws a large crowd, so we arrived an hour and a half early to make sure we snagged good seats. I pull out a chair and sit down across from them. "They have terrible valet service here," I say. "They make you ride with them, and then they give you your keys. So all they're really offering is to show you where to park."

"That's not true valet service," my mom says.

"And the guy was really rude to me—he kept ordering me to go with him. I finally said to Murray, '*You* go, I'm not going.'"

My parents look back at me sadly but don't respond. They are used to people finding fault with their city. Sometimes my parents defend Detroit, and other times they keep quiet.

I take off my coat and drape it on the back of my chair. Cliff Bell's is a fancier place than I thought it would be—brass rails by the bar; classy, dark wood trim; low, elegant lighting. Each of the waitresses wears a different style of dress, all of them edgy and hip yet somehow sophisticated. The young black bouncer watching over the bar has on a blue and yellow silk jacket, and the young white man greeting patrons at the door, in addition to his black suit and round black hat, sports trendy, thin strips of dark beard along his jaw line and retro, thick-framed black glasses. Judging by the valet I expected that Cliff Bell's would be more of a dive.

"What would you like to drink?" my dad asks. "We should order wine for Murray, right?"

"Chardonnay for Murray," I say. "I'll have water for now."

A waitress stops to take our orders. As she speaks with my mom and dad my thoughts return to the valet. Besides being rude, he was extremely unprofessional. An image returns to me: my last sight of the valet, his angry profile as he drove off with his skinny cigar clamped between his lips. A lot of people don't like you to smoke in their cars, I think. The word *unprofessional* comes to mind again. Then the image returns, as vivid as a snapshot: the man's angry face, and Murray, in the dark beyond him, mostly obscured—more a sense of him than a sight. I couldn't see Murray well enough to tell if he was worried or frightened. I look up from the table and around the dark room with a disturbing thought: maybe the valet looked unprofessional because he *wasn't* a valet. Even without the half-burnt cigar, he seemed kind of disheveled. What if he's just some guy on the street, unconnected to Cliff Bell's, out there scamming people or even robbing them? Murray has been gone for ten or fifteen minutes. A lot could happen in that time. My car might be stolen; Murray could be lying in the street somewhere. An even darker thought crosses my mind: what if my last, blurry sight of Murray is my last sight of him ever?

"I'm wondering if that guy wasn't really a valet," I say to my parents. They stare back at me as if they don't quite know what to say. Each time I visit them, they seem older and smaller. I explain my doubts. Then I say, "I'm going to find out," and I stand and walk toward the man in the black suit and hat greeting patrons at the door.

⊙

I've taken only a few steps when Murray strides in through the door, obviously stirred up but unhurt. Towering above the manager, he points behind him at the street. I hurry toward Murray, but slow down a few feet off, stopping outside the perimeter of his agitation.

"Your valet," Murray says, "your valet is doing an incredibly lousy job."

The manager looks at Murray blankly.

"Is that your valet out there?" Murray demands.

The bouncer, whose muscles fill out his blue and yellow silk jacket, has sidled up next to the manager. He and the manager exchange hesitant looks. Then the manager speaks. "We have a valet. But he's not here yet. He's not due for another fifteen minutes."

"Well, there's someone out there parking cars for you and he nearly fucking killed me driving around the block."

"What?"

"There's some guy out there claiming to be your valet and he's crazy and he charged me twenty bucks. I got in the car with him, and he tore off down the street with his foot to the floor. Then he went racing down this alley, swerving all over the place, almost ramming a dumpster, barely missing buildings and fences."

"What does he look like?" the manager asks.

"He's about my height and he's scruffy, with a cigar dangling from his mouth."

I speak up from the edge of their circle. "He tried to make me go with him," I say. "He kept saying, 'She needs to go with me.'"

The manager looks at me, and his pale face darkens. "We'll take care of him," he says grimly, pulling on his coat. He isn't nearly as tall as Murray or the wannabe valet, and his hat, beard, and glasses look a little goofy, but the determination in his voice and his youthfulness seem like they might make up for his lack of stature and his costume.

I return to my parents, and the manager and the bouncer walk outside with Murray. Ten minutes later, Murray comes back in and joins us at our table. "We found him," Murray says. "He was back out there, trying to park another car. The club guys tried to get the twenty back from him, but he insisted he didn't have it. Started pulling bills out of his pockets, and all he came up with was seven dollars. They said it wasn't legal for them to shake him down, so they called the police."

"Are the police coming?" I ask.

"They're out there right now."

Murray picks up his wineglass and takes a slug. "I thought we were going to crash for sure. I thought there was no way we wouldn't crash." I rub Murray's thigh, and he pats my hand. "It happened so fast," he says. He leans across the table to include my parents. "You should have seen this guy. First he floors it and tries to swerve into an alley, but he misses and plows right into a huge snowdrift. He keeps gunning the engine, as if he's going to drive right through the drift. I tell him he has to put it in reverse, and he starts fumbling with the shift. 'I don't know how to work this thing,' he says. So I pull it into reverse for him, and he starts spinning the wheels like crazy, burning down to the pavement. Finally, he manages to get unstuck from the drift. But then he blasts off down the alley, just missing this giant dumpster, almost hitting a row of garbage cans, fishtailing back and forth between all these buildings and a half mile of chain-link fence. I'm asking him, 'Where are you going? What are you doing?' And he keeps saying, as if it were obvious, 'I'm taking you to your spot. I've got the perfect spot for you, man, all picked out.'

"Finally we shoot out of the alley, spin a three-sixty in the street, and then he punches the accelerator again, and we take off at sixty miles an hour and swerve again and fly across this empty parking lot and slide to a stop beside an empty parking booth.

"'See?' he says. 'Here it is. Your spot.'

"I say, 'Yeah, thanks a lot, man,' and I get out of the car.

"And he says, 'Hey, man, don't forget to pay me.'

"I say, 'We already paid you,' and he says, 'No, you didn't.' I say, 'We paid you twenty dollars,' and he says, 'You paid me, but you took it back. And it's thirty dollars—see?' And he points up at a sign above the parking booth that says: Parking—All Day—$30.

"I tell him he's gotten his twenty and that's already too much, and I start walking away. And he starts crying out in this pathetic voice, 'Man, don't leave me! Don't leave me here! My knees, my knees—I can't get out!'

"So I turn back around, and I notice that the man's knees are jammed up under the steering wheel because the seat's still adjusted for Annie. And he's crying like a little kid, 'Please don't leave me here—don't leave me!' So I walk back to him and push on the lever, and the seat glides back. And he gets out of the car and closes the door and says, 'You still need to pay me, man.'

"I say, 'You got your twenty dollars, and that's all you're getting.'

"And he starts whining, 'She paid me, but you took it back! She paid me, but you took it back!'

"I just walked away. Meanwhile he's shouting, 'Don't cheat me, man! Don't lie to me! You owe me!'"

Murray shakes his head and lifts his wineglass and takes another slug.

"What about my car?" I ask.

"It's fine," Murray says. "Miraculously, not a scratch."

"Does it need to be moved?"

"No, the lot it's in is empty, closed for the night."

"Are you sure it won't get towed?"

"I showed the club guys where it is, and they say it's fine." He lifts his glass as if toasting. "I'm going to need another couple of these, though, to help me settle down."

I slide my arm across Murray's broad back and lean my head against his arm, soaking up his warmth and solidity, reveling in his palpable presence while at the same time feeling guilty. "I feel so bad that I sent you off with that guy."

"Don't worry about it," Murray says, as usual not wanting to make a fuss.

"He could have robbed you. He could have had a knife, or a gun."

"Don't worry about it. It's over with."

Across the table from us, my parents have the same sad, troubled looks on their faces as when I complained to them a year ago about Detroit. The expressway leading to downtown had been closed for repairs, so we had to take the city streets in, through mile after mile of rough neighborhoods, past abandoned, burned-out, or simply crumbling houses and boarded-up storefronts, block after block where the only viable businesses were liquor stores and bars. Night had fallen, and shadowy men stood out in front of the bars, even though it was winter. A Hummer with tinted windows tailed us through a dozen traffic lights. Finally, it turned off onto a side street, but by then I wasn't sure where we were anymore, and I'd started to panic. I'd been attacked by a mob of girls one winter day when I was growing up in Detroit, and even though that was decades ago and I escaped being badly hurt, the fear I felt at being knocked down and clawed at and dragged down the street still returns to me at times, in an instant.

"Why do you still live in this place?" I asked my parents

after we finally arrived at their condo. "It makes me mad that in order to come see you, we have to risk our safety. If our car had broken down in one of those neighborhoods, we'd have been dead meat."

My mom and dad kept as quiet then as they are now. But as we sit at the table in Cliff Bell's, I don't say anything about Detroit being dangerous. I don't want to make my parents feel any worse than they already do. Except for that one time, I've never complained about returning to my home city. Although my feelings about Detroit are definitely mixed, I still love coming back to visit.

⊙

Cliff Bell's is offering a buffet, and after Murray has soothed his nerves with a second glass of wine, we stand up and fill our plates with ribs, chicken, salad, and mac and cheese. A friend of my parents joins us, and Murray tells him about his ride with the wannabe valet. Murray's story grows a little with the second telling—this time, instead of the car doing only one three-sixty spin, after exiting the alley, Murray adds another full-circle spin, right before the car comes to a stop below the thirty-dollar-a-day parking sign. Once when I admonished Murray for exaggerating—he told his mom that the snow in his yard was all the way up to our thighs when really it only reached to my calves—his middle son said, "Well, we all know the Dad exaggeration equation: divide by half."

After we've eaten, I approach the manager. "Did you get my twenty back?" I ask him.

He shakes his round-hatted head. "Not yet. But we're working on it."

"Did you find out anything else?"

"Not so far—we turned the homeless guy over to the police."

"He's homeless?"

"Yeah, I believe so," the manager says, trying not to show that he thinks I'm naïve.

"I thought he looked kind of disheveled for a valet," I say.

"Did he say he was a valet?" the manager asks.

"I don't remember. He said something about parking my car, and that it cost twenty dollars."

The manager continues to look at me as if trying not to reveal what he thinks.

"I was trying to get my dad into the club, and things were kind of confusing, with all the snow in the street, so when this guy walked up to my window, I assumed he was your valet. I can't remember if he said he was. He just asked for twenty dollars and my keys."

The manager nods, trying unsuccessfully to hide his incredulity, not wanting to appear impolite. We stare at each other for a moment without speaking.

"Well, I grew up in Detroit," I explain, "but I've lived out in the country for a long time."

⊙

James Carter and Hot Club of Detroit start off their show with a rocketing blast, all of the quintet and Carter in sync and fired up. It's hard to believe it's the first song of their first set—they sound as if they've been jamming all night. No wonder they call themselves Hot Club of Detroit, even though, except for the sax, what they play don't seem like the hottest of instruments: two acoustic guitars, an upright bass, and a button accordion. James Carter stands at their center, playing sax also, his golden horn flashing as he bobs and sways. Carter is black—a deep, dark, velvety brown—and the Hot Club of Detroit are various shades of white. Jazz musicians have always shared a kind of ease with each other, a color-blind understanding that is rare among the general public, and as the six of them play together, trading riffs, handing off solos, they are grinning and joking like cousins at a family reunion. But I'm not feeling relaxed, and after that first song, I have trouble focusing on the music. I'll be enjoying an incredible sax riff or an intricate guitar solo, and then my thoughts will return to the wannabe valet. I wonder if he would have tried to rape me if I had driven off with him. But probably he simply figured that, since I'd been dumb enough to give him twenty dollars, he might be able to milk me for another ten.

Now that I've had time to think about it, I can see that the man looked homeless. But only *potentially* homeless—he didn't have that filthy and severely disturbed look of an end-stage alcoholic or seriously mentally ill homeless person.

My adopted hometown of Saugatuck, where I've lived for more than thirty years, has hosted only one homeless man that I know of, a one-armed artist who lived in a tent by the river for several seasons before taking off for Colorado. But I've seen a lot of panhandlers and homeless people in Detroit, more and more over the years, at the Eastern Market and in Greektown, by the riverfront and on all the other streets around my parents' condo. Sometimes I'll give one a dollar or two, but more often I'll look away from eyes so tired and worn, so filmed over or deranged, that it's hard to meet let alone hold their gazes. This year, as part of my Christmas present to my parents, instead of donating another sheep, pig, or llama in their name to a family in a foreign country, I decided to give closer to home, and I wrote out a check to Detroit's oldest soup kitchen. As I face the stage, tapping my feet, watching James Carter ease the mouth of his horn up to the mike and then draw slowly back, controlling horn, hands, lips, and breath perfectly to milk out the sweetest notes, I wonder if the wannabe valet ever eats at that soup kitchen, if part of my money will provide him with a meal. I think of how he demanded I go with him, and I imagine taking his soup bowl from his hands and throwing it in his face. But that image dissolves as quickly as it appears. He didn't hurt me, or Murray, either, and even homeless scammers deserve to eat.

⊙

On our last trip in to my hometown, in front of the Detroit Institute of Arts, a woman asked me for money. Murray had stopped after we left the museum to take some close-up photos of the building. Sometimes I complain when Murray turns a brisk walk or vacation outing into a photo expedition, but that day I paced up and down the sidewalk to pass the time while he stepped close to the building's perimeter and angled and shot. I'd walked up and down the block three times when a woman approached me from behind and off to my right. "Miss," she called softly. "Miss—I need your help."

I turned toward her and stopped.

"I know what I need to do," the woman said, "but I need your help."

"What kind of help do you need?" I asked, looking at

her as closely as I'd just gazed at Van Gogh's portraits. Her skin was very dark, and she was built small, like me. She was also like me in that she wore no makeup and her clothes were extremely casual: faded jeans, a worn tan coat (mine is black), and scuffed leather athletic shoes. The main difference in our dress was that she had no hat or gloves. She looked like she *could* be a panhandler or homeless. But not necessarily.

"I need to get to the battered women's shelter," she said. "I know where it is, and I know how to get there, but I need five dollars for bus fare for my children and me. It's a dollar fifty for me, plus three more for my children."

I looked into her dark face, into her eyes. I've never been good at telling if a person is drunk or high. Or lying.

As I stared at her, she said, "See these bruises?" She traced her skin right below both eyes. It was slightly darker there, but whether from bruises or from lack of sleep or other hard luck, it wasn't clear.

I used to volunteer two nights a month for a domestic abuse crisis line, and I'd heard plenty of stories from abused women who were ignored or not believed. I reached into my coat pocket and pulled out my wallet. All I had were two singles and two twenties. As I started to pull out a twenty, her eyes flickered. I paused, looking beyond her, up the street. "Where are your children?" I asked. All I could see were college students and other adults.

"I left them at the library," she said. "They're waiting there for me."

I hesitated another second. Then I slipped out the bill and held it out to her. She took it, said, "Oh, thank you," and turned away. The woman started strolling up the street toward the corner, walking more slowly, it seemed, than someone in a hurry to get back to her children and transport them and herself to safety. Either she was half dazed, unable to believe her and her children's good luck, or she couldn't believe her own, solitary good luck and was trying to decide whether to buy wine, whiskey, heroin, or some of each.

I would rather chance wasting twenty dollars on an addict than turn my back on a battered woman, yet I still wanted to know whether or not I had been fooled, so when Murray rejoined me, I told him what had happened and asked if he thought she was telling the truth.

"From what you've said, I can't tell."

"Well, what do you think the *chances* are that she was telling the truth?" I pressed.

"I'd say about fifty-fifty."

I wondered if Murray was lying to be nice. "Are you just saying that to make me feel better?"

He frowned. "I don't know, Annie. It's impossible to say."

"It's impossible to say whether she was telling the truth, or whether you are?"

He smiled and said, "Both."

A few days before this, in one of our rare arguments, Murray had complained about what he calls my obsession with the truth. He had asked me to meet him early for dinner and then had kept me waiting for a half hour, and we were in disagreement about the surrounding facts. Finally I had said, "I just want you to admit that you were wrong."

He had answered, "I wasn't *wrong,* I was *late.* And why is it important?"

"Because I like to get the facts straight."

"Jesus, you're supposed to be a freaking fiction writer."

"And you're supposed to be a photographer! The most true-to-life type of art."

"What are you talking about?" he had said. "Photography is the greatest fiction there is! It's all about angles and lighting and tricks."

"Well, fiction is mainly about telling the truth."

"Why does one person have to be right?" Murray had asked. "What if both of us are right? What if both of us are wrong?"

I had kept quiet, pondering what might be the right and truthful answers to these questions.

⊙

James Carter and Hot Club of Detroit finish their first set with "Summertime," despite, or perhaps *to* spite, all the snow piled up outside. The acoustic guitars and the accordion, which make me think of a campfire, cause the song to sound like a cross between "Summertime" and "Home on the Range." It is an odd yet pleasant hybrid.

After it's over, we stand up to leave. I tell Murray that I want the real valet, the club's valet, to retrieve our car for us.

"No, we've had enough bother," Murray says, pulling on his coat. "I'll get it. It's right around the corner from here."

"But what if that guy is out there? He could be waiting at our car, mad at us because we called the police on him."

"He won't be out there," Murray says. "The police hauled him off."

"They did? Are you sure?"

"Yes. I saw them put the handcuffs on."

"Were they black or white?"

"The police?"

"Yes."

"One of each, I think."

I feel somewhat relieved, although I know a cop being black doesn't guarantee he'll be humane. And though the man who scammed us has been hauled off, that doesn't mean the streets are safe now. "I'm going with you," I tell Murray. "I'm walking with you to get the car." I don't want to let him out of my sight. If someone else tries to take him for a ride, they'll have to deal with me, too. I'm small, but I can be fierce.

On our way out the door, I ask the manager, "Did you get my twenty back?"

"No," he says. "We weren't able to. Sorry."

"Well, what about the seven dollars you got from him?" I ask. "Can you give me that?"

The manager ducks his round-hatted head and shifts his eyes away. "He said the seven dollars was his own money, so we gave it back to him."

"You gave it back to him?"

"Yes. He said it was his." He glances at me again. "We told him we'd give him back his seven if he gave us the twenty." He lowers his voice. "And then he wouldn't give us the twenty."

I look at him as he looked at me earlier in the evening, when I told him I've lived out in the country for a long time.

⊙

Holding hands, Murray and I make our way down the snowy, slushy street. I'm still a little worried that something bad might happen before we reach my car. After all, we are walking in Detroit at night, and if we could run into trouble once, why not twice? That I'm alert now to possible danger isn't much solace. Whenever I've made a dumb move, afterward I always reassure myself that I won't make that mistake again. Next time I won't hand my keys over to a scruffy stranger, or send the love of my life off into the night with a madman. But the problem with this reasoning is that the next time is always different.

Rounding a corner, I see my car, the only car in the lot, lined up at surprisingly right angles to the street and looking reassuringly fine: whole and unmolested despite its brief, wild spin. Overhead is the sign Murray mentioned: Parking—All Day—$30.

I click the remote to unlock the car and open the driver's door. As I'm about to step in, I notice a folded-up bill on the driver's seat. "Murray," I call. "Come here—look at this."

Murray cozies up to my side. I point down at the bill. "Look what I found. Lying right there."

Murray reaches in, picks up the bill, and unfolds it. It's a twenty. "So he *was* telling the truth," Murray says.

"The truth!"

"Well, part of the truth," Murray amends.

He hands me the bill, and I slip it into my pocket. Then Murray says, "Damn!"

I glance around us, alert, but all I see are the still city streets, empty except for the waves of snow and slush. "What?" I ask.

"I should have taken a photo of him! I had my camera in my coat pocket the whole time."

⊙

We pick up my parents at the door of the club, and then Murray has me stop the car at the alley he was taken down, and he gets out and takes some pictures of the ruts carved in the snow as my car veered toward a massive metal dumpster, angling away just in time, cutting more curves as it fishtailed up the alley. I peer as far as I can up the dark, snowy corridor, trying to see to the alley's far end; I'm attempting to discern the marks of a three-sixty spin, but it's too dark and distant to tell what's there and what isn't.

On the drive home, the four of us are laughing, light-hearted. The whole night has tipped from potential or averted disaster to a comedy of errors. "Look at it this way," my mom says. "You got a thirty-dollar parking spot for free." Then she tells a story about my sister, who lives in a suburb that borders Detroit and is regularly approached by homeless men on her trips into the city. Nicole has taken to giving them whatever food she has in her car. When a homeless man approaches her window at a red light, she'll grab whatever she has—candy, crackers, cookies—roll down the window, and say, "Here."

Recently, Nicole and her husband were returning home from our parents' condo with two loaves of German *stollen* that my mom had made for Nicole's husband's family. Nicole grabbed up one of the round loaves from the backseat as a homeless man approached.

"You can't give that away," her husband objected. "It's a Christmas present. And not *your* Christmas present."

Nicole rolled down her window, held out the bread, and said, "Here."

The man looked down at the foil-covered round loaf that Nicole thrust into his hands. "What is it?" he asked.

"It's stollen," Nicole said.

"It's *stolen*?" the man asked.

"Yes," Nicole said. "Take it. It's for you."

Looking stricken, the man backed off from the car window holding the loaf on his open hands as if it might be a bomb.

We laugh at this story, and then we laugh some more at the events of the evening. But as I look out at the lights of downtown, at the radiant glow of the Renaissance Center and the flashing neon of Greektown, my thoughts darken. I see the homeless man, our valet, being questioned at the station, insisting to the police that he isn't telling a story, that he doesn't have the twenty and he hasn't stashed it anywhere. I know that they don't believe him, and I am hoping they haven't mistreated him, trying to get at the truth.

I'll Be
Your
Witness

I ran into Delia last night at the corner store near my house. She walked up behind me and touched my arm while I was waiting in the checkout line. "Tiff!" she said. "Girl, you look just the same!" I didn't tell her that almost everyone calls me Tiffany now. It felt kind of good hearing my old nickname from Delia. But I also felt a pang, as if Tiff and Dee-Dee were girls we'd known who had died.

Delia's voice had gathered rust in the ten years since I had last seen her. Her body had widened from scrawny to average, and she'd dyed her blond hair bright blue and cut most of it off. "You still living in Highland Park?" she asked.

Highland Park, where we grew up, is a little city inside Detroit. Struggling even when we were young girls, Highland Park has since fallen on far harder times.

"No, I'm here in Ferndale now," I told her.

"Good for you!" she said. "So what else is new? What you been up to? Married? Got a job?"

"Not married," I said. "I'm working at the Ferndale Library."

"Tiff the librarian!" Delia said. "Wouldn't you know it. Meanwhile I'm selling beer—and mopping it up from the floor." She laughed and made a face. Delia explained she was working at a bar on Nine Mile, the Stop Spot Lounge, a few blocks from where we stood. I'd seen it, but like most bars, dive or otherwise, I'd never been inside it.

We made our purchases—Delia bought cigarettes and a fifth of whiskey; I bought a quart of orange juice—and then we moved our conversation outside. It was a cold November day, but Delia stood with her vinyl jacket unzipped. She told me she'd moved back to Highland Park a month ago, after her second divorce. I hadn't heard about the first divorce or her second marriage—all I'd known was that Dee had eloped to Ohio ten years ago when she was seventeen, long after our friendship was over, and shortly after that her mom and her brothers had moved out of the city, too. I'd spent my own time away: six and a half years at college in East Lansing, living with roommates and then my boyfriend and then with just my tortoise and my cat. But all I told Dee was that my mom had moved from our old house in Highland Park into a Southfield apartment, and that I'm renting a small house in Ferndale that I'm hoping to buy.

"You should come down to see *my* house," Delia said. "Well, it's not really mine. Belongs to my new boyfriend. Or new ex-boyfriend. Whatever, you should see the crazy place he built. It's in Highland Park, but on the other side of Woodward from where we grew up."

"Maybe I will sometime," I said, taking a step backward down the cold sidewalk, hunching my shoulders against the wind.

"Okay," Delia said. "It's been great seeing ya! Keep in touch."

"It was good seeing you, too," I said, which was partly the truth.

Ordinarily things would have ended there, as chance encounters with past friends mostly do. If we ran into each other again, she'd have said: *We should get together.* And the next time, if there was a next time: *We really should get together!* And then we never would.

The truth is, I'm not like most people when it comes to being social—I prefer spending my free time with books. With people there's just too much chaff—a person might say one interesting thing in an entire hour—whereas with books, at least the good ones, they're engaging page after page. And if I change my mind about a book, I can put it down with no hurt feelings. I do try sometimes to be more social. At my job, for instance, and I also volunteer at Ferndale Elementary, listening to first-graders read. In the evenings, though, I'd rather be alone, with no one for company except Flannery my cat and Alice my tortoise, both of whom are quiet and serene.

But after Delia and I said good-bye, I couldn't get my car to start. My used Escort—all I can afford on my librarian's salary—has turned out to be a piece of junk.

"Hey," Delia said. She'd pulled up alongside me and was leaning out the window of a battered Jeep.

I looked up and over at her, my hands gripping the wheel. Then I tried the starter again.

"Girl," Delia said, "if it ain't turned over by now, it ain't gonna. Hop in. I'll run you home."

"It's not far," I said. "I can walk."

Delia's eyes did that thing that people's eyes do when they realize they're being shut out. It's as if a clear but impenetrable glass shield slips down. This had happened before with me and Dee, when we were twelve. I wanted to stop it from happening again. Except for my ex-boyfriend, Dee is the only close friend I've ever had.

"Wait a minute," I said, and I scrambled out from behind the wheel, grabbed my jug of juice, and hurried around to the Jeep's passenger door. Delia leaned across and let me in.

When I'd got myself situated on the high seat, she glanced at my hand clutching the jug's plastic loop. "Well, you're all set for the evening," she joked. "Kinda hard to tip and swig, though, ain't it?"

I smiled, and, wanting to act as if I wasn't the same staid person she'd left behind, I uncapped the jug and tipped it back, feeling silly yet proud as the cold juice went down that I could drink like that and not choke.

Dee laughed. She's got this laugh I've always envied: loud and happy, head thrown back. My laughter is soft and stilted, if I laugh at all. Sometimes, to let people know I get the joke, I'll say, *That's funny*.

"Mind if I smoke?" Delia asked.

"No," I lied.

"Good," Delia said, "since it's my truck." She laughed again, and lit a cigarette. "How about," she said, shifting into gear, "'fore I run you home, I take you down to Highland Park to see my house? You don't have a hot date tonight, do you?"

"No," I said. I hadn't had a date of any sort since college, and even then, they were hardly dates—just my boyfriend and me hanging out together, eating endless bowls of ramen noodles.

"You've never seen a house like this one," Delia said. She threw the spent match out her window; as she worked the cigarette pack back into her purse, I tried to think of a polite way to decline. Then she grinned right at me and said, "Or *read* about one like it, either."

Her words zoomed me back to when we were kids: Dee-Dee pounding up the stairs, throwing open my door. She knew where to find me—on my bed or in summer on the floor, always reading. "C'mon, Tiff," she'd say. "Let's *do* something."

Sometimes we'd go down to the kitchen and fix something to eat: Kraft mac and cheese, or a Kool-Aid cake—our own invention. Or we'd beg a few quarters from my mom to spend on candy at Ali's. Or we'd just set off, without quarters or a destination, searching the streets and alleys for whatever we could find: mulberries, empty pop cans, baby birds fallen from their nests. People always said, "You ain't sisters? You look just like sisters." Because we were white and always together, I guess, and we had the same thin bodies and same long, straight, thin hair, though Dee-Dee's was dark blond and mine was dark brown.

Now Delia flicked her short blue hair out of her face. "So, what do you say?" she asked. "Want to see my new place? You don't have to worry about crime—almost everyone has left Highland Park, including the criminals!"

I looked out through the windshield at the gray street, feeling the cold orange juice through the plastic against my skin. "Sure," I said. Flannery and Alice could eat a little later for once, and so could I; my chicken chili and new Atwood novel could wait.

"I'm not gonna drive past our old houses," Delia said. "Yours is boarded up, and the roof is falling in—did you know that?"

I told her I didn't; I hadn't gone back to look.

"And mine," she said, "mine isn't there at all anymore."

Delia drove east on Nine Mile, then south on Woodward Avenue, which was packed on both sides with trendy shops and upscale restaurants and bars. Crossing Eight Mile, we passed out of Ferndale and into Detroit. The businesses here were fewer and older, with empty, abandoned spaces between them; then came the closed-down fairgrounds on our left and Palmer Park on our right. Driving further south, we crossed Six Mile, and then we were in Highland Park. First we passed a cluster of adult theaters and bars, then a Glory Grocery and a tire store. Just past the viaduct was the first factory Henry Ford ever built—closed for decades, it was still standing, though a lot of its windows were broken. Then Delia turned off Woodward onto a side street. I expected to see plenty of boarded-up houses—although I've only ventured into Highland Park once since I left, I've seen photos and news clips—but what surprised me was how many houses were totally gone. We'd pass a few blocks where the single houses and two-family flats were in various stages of decay—along with a number that were fairly well kept—and then there'd be a block, or even two, with no houses at all. When we reached

Delia's current street, at the end of the first block, there was a cluster of four or five well-cared-for homes, with mowed lawns and scrolled burglar bars covering the windows on the first floors. But up and down the rest of the street, there wasn't a house in sight, and what had once been individual lots had blurred into a single vast field.

It had grown dark since we'd set out. There were no streetlights and, without houses, no porch lights, but there was enough moonlight to see by. In the middle of the second block, Delia brought the Jeep to a stop. The weeds rose high, brown and brittle, and the street and the sidewalk were almost entirely rubble. Here and there, a few scrub trees had grown fairly tall—trees-of-heaven with their angular branches, clumps of sumac with dark red horns. "Cozy little house in the middle of nowhere," Delia said. She looked at my puzzled face and laughed. "It's built underground, like a bunker," she explained. "Remember Chuck Slater?"

I shook my head.

"Neither do I," Delia said, and laughed again. "He was ten years ahead of us at school. But, well, when I got up here, I was living with my aunt, looking for a better place, and Chuck invited me to stay with him." She lit another cigarette. The Jeep idled in the road. "I wasn't here but a week when Chuck took off—up north somewhere, to join a survivalist group. I'm trying not to take it personally."

She pulled the Jeep up to the disintegrating curb and turned it off, and we clumped through rubble and dead weeds and brush to a steel door leading down into the ground. "Kinda creepy," Delia said. "But safe." She smirked. "That is, unless Chuckie comes back. Oh, don't worry, he wouldn't hurt *you*, Tiff. Or me, either. But trespassers? Watch out. He's kind of paranoid. Couple months ago, he shot this big fat groundhog, swore the government had had it bugged. Sliced that poor animal into a hundred pieces looking for the hidden microphone."

"I didn't know there were groundhogs living in the city," I said.

Delia snorted. "You call this a city? They turned off the streetlights. They turned off the water! They closed down the high school and threw out all the books."

I'd heard about that—it was all over the news. Even the United Nations had gotten involved, as if Highland Park and Detroit were third world countries. Most but not all of the shut-off houses had running water again, but a lot of the streetlights were still dark, and others had been removed, lampposts and all. Thousands of books, including irreplaceable ones on Highland Park and Black History, had been thrown like rags into a dumpster. Some but not all of those books had been rescued by a local historian.

Delia looked around at the weeds rising up all around us with a twisted smile and said, "Chuck should invite his survivalist pals to move down here." Then she unlocked the metal door and pulled it open, and we walked down cement stairs into a central room, and from there into a room Delia called "the pantry." It was constructed of cement blocks and lined with shelves stacked with cans: mostly beef stew, but also kidney beans and ravioli. And there was one whole wall of Kraft mac and cheese, with gaps here and there like missing bricks where boxes had been removed. "Grab a box," Delia said. "Oh, c'mon, take one from the bottom."

I pulled one out slowly, without bringing the wall down, and Delia cheered and clapped.

We fixed the macaroni like we did when we were girls, taking turns with all the steps, but we had to use a gas-powered hot plate to cook the elbows and mix in powdered milk instead of fresh. Then Delia opened her fifth, and though I rarely drink—you know people like me, the maybe-a-glass-of-wine-with-dinner types—I took a swig and then some more. I couldn't help shuddering and shaking my head like a cat whose face has gotten wet. But I liked how it felt warm in my throat and then glowed like a small fire all the way down to my belly.

We ate mac and cheese and talked about old times: "Remember when we were coloring on the floor in your bedroom," Dee said, "and the door was off its hinges, and one of us nudged it, and it came crashing down on our heads?"

"One of us?" I repeated.

"Girl, don't blame it on me," Dee said with a smile. She stabbed another bite of the neon orange elbows and washed them down with whiskey. "Remember when I shoplifted those two bikinis," she said, "and then ditched them behind a counter before the store dick could find them on me, and he didn't believe you when you said you hadn't taken either one? Remember that?"

"Yeah, sure," I said, unable to keep from smiling, too, although my feelings about stirring up the past like this were mixed.

"And then when your ma came to pick us up," Delia said, "the dick told her that the blonde—me—seemed to regret what she had done, 'but the dark-haired one, she's a hard case, I'd watch her if I were you.'" We laughed, but I felt something like a shadow stretch across my inner vision. I'd forgotten the detective's warning, but now his words rang true, except that the dark thing in me that needed watching had turned inward.

"Speaking of trouble," Delia said as if reading my mind, "what about men? What's the story on that?"

"No story," I said, looking down at the backs of my hands, at the table, at the bright orange elbow noodles glowing in the light thrown by a small lantern. Delia waited for more, but I kept quiet. I've had only the one boyfriend, the one in college, and when he left me after two years, I went into a downward spiral from which I didn't think I'd recover. First I stopped going to classes. Then I stopped eating meals. Then I even stopped reading the books that had always been my solace.

"You're right," Delia said at last. "*Men*. We should save our breath on that topic."

We talked some more about old times, and we finished the macaroni, and Delia finished the whiskey. Then we climbed back up out of the ground, and she drove me home in one piece. "Keep in touch!" she yelled from her Jeep as I opened my front door, making Alice scrabble for a corner and Flannery streak from the room.

⊙

Now it's morning, and I'm standing in the kitchen of the house I'm renting and hoping to own, a vinyl-sided house with its four walls above ground, surrounded by other tidy houses and mowed lawns for blocks around, and here comes Delia, striding up my walk. As soon as I see her, my heart sinks. Tiff and Dee-Dee are dead, and I don't think I want to try to revive them. Neither do I want to start over from here.

But Delia's on my front stoop, and what else can I do? I open the door and let her in.

"Girl," she says right off, "I need you for a character witness."

"Want something to drink?" I ask. "Though all I have are coffee and juice."

"I'm all set," Delia says, easing onto the couch and slipping a flask from her purse. She's wearing a short, black crepe skirt with a pink leotard and tights, red bra straps jutting from the leotard's scoop neck. On someone else it would look crazy and cheap, but on Delia it comes off as stylish and cute. "You know what I just found out?" she says, taking a sip. "I'm pregnant again."

"You are?" I say stupidly, wondering what she means by "again." She didn't mention any children last night, and I saw no evidence of any at her ex-boyfriend's bunker. But of course, abortion or miscarriage could account for that.

"No lie," she says. "About seven weeks along."

"You shouldn't be drinking," I say, surprising myself by speaking up.

"You're right," Delia says. She stands, her skirt rustling against her tights. "Where's your sink?"

I look around to make sure Alice isn't underfoot. That's another reason I don't like guests—people are blundering and don't watch where they step. But Alice is smart: she has tucked herself out of sight and is probably also closed up inside her shell.

I lead Delia to the kitchen, feeling like a modern-day Carrie Nation. She upends the flask over the sink and says, "My whole life is going down the drain." Her bracelets rattle like chattering teeth as she shakes the bottle dry. Then she straightens up, flips her hair out of her face, and says, "I need to get my child back."

"Back from where?" I ask. *What child?* I think.

"A home," Delia says. "A place in Ohio. Where they put him when he was four."

"A foster home?" I ask.

"Sort of," Delia says. "A mental foster home. Kind of like a hospital."

It feels like a stone is pressing my heart down. I was taken to a psychiatric hospital after my boyfriend broke up with me. Had to miss a semester of college. I cover the scar—there's just one, I chickened out after the first cut—with a wide watchband or long sleeves. Even when I'm alone, I keep it covered.

"They say he's autistic," Delia says. "He doesn't like to talk or for people to get too close. But he *knows* how to talk—he *does*, sometimes. He's got dark hair, these big, brown eyes. Likes to play basketball, by himself." Delia's blue hair slants into her face as she paws through her purse. We're still standing in the kitchen next to the sink. She pulls a school photo from her wallet and hands it to me. Her boy has beautiful, dark eyes and a subdued but not wholly vacant expression. She takes the photo back and slips it into her wallet, then fingers a pack of cigarettes but doesn't take one out. "He's eight now," Delia says. "Someone adopted him last year, but a couple months ago, they gave him back."

"*They gave him back?*"

"Had the adoption annulled," Delia says, tapping the pack of cigarettes against her skirted thigh.

"They can do that?" I ask.

Delia laughs instead of answering. Then she says, "Jesus, maybe I will have some of that juice. Pretend there's vodka in it."

I get out a water glass and pour it full. As Delia opens her mouth to drink, I notice a dark spot, an untreated cavity, on the left side of her mouth. She takes the glass from her lips and repeats what she said when she first walked in: "I need you for a character witness. To testify in court."

"For what?" I ask, thinking of drunk driving or maybe drugs, not making the connection yet.

"To get my kid back," Delia explains. She frowns at the glass of juice in her hand.

I think of keeping quiet as usual, but then I don't. Maybe I'm remembering that when we were girls, Delia was the one person besides my mom I could really talk to. "I think you should leave your first kid where he is," I say, "at least until you're more . . . stabilized. I think you should focus on this other kid for now."

Delia looks at me as if we are strangers. Of course, we didn't talk about stuff like this when we were girls. "Stabilized," she repeats. "What do you mean by that?" She's staring at me but her eyes are nearly squinted closed. I realize that I don't really know her anymore.

"Dee," I say, "remember those little birds we always used to try to save?"

Nothing registers in her brittle face.

"Little pink, baby birds with their wrinkled, wobbly necks? With those bulging, purple eyes that weren't open yet?"

"Yeah, so?" Delia says.

"How many ever lived?"

"What is this, a science quiz? We're not talking about

birds, we're talking about my boy. Besides, if anything's a baby bird, it's this one here," she says, pressing the puckered black crepe beneath the waistband of her skirt. "If anything, we should forget about this one, not Henry."

Henry. He has a name.

I look down at my kitchen floor, which I usually walk across without a care. There's no one to trip me up—Alice doesn't like to crawl on vinyl, and Flannery steers clear of me unless I'm opening a can. They've both disappeared now and won't come out—they're unused to strangers and loud talking.

But now Delia is standing in front of me, waiting, blocking my path. "So," she says, "will you come to court with me and be my witness?"

I glance up at her and glance away. Today is Sunday, my one day off. All I want to do is read my new novel, look at the paper, lie around with my cat. Not answer questions. Not make promises or plans.

Delia's still staring at me with her eyes narrowed tight. I look at the old blue glass bottles lined up on my kitchen window, wishing she had never come over. Not to this comfortable little fortress. Not to the decrepit two-story I lived in when we were girls.

"Well, I need a smoke," Delia says. Her eyes relax and droop—they look tired and also wet. She picks up her purse from the counter, slings it over her shoulder, and straightens the neck of her leotard, tucking a red bra strap out of sight.

I'll be your witness.

I say it in my head; I don't let the words out. I want to make things right between us. But I also don't want Delia to stay in my house.

She walks a beeline through my living room, goes out my front door, and hurries down my four concrete steps without a word. Halfway across my front yard, she stops and strikes a match and holds it to her cigarette, inhaling until it's lit. Then she resumes her brisk pace without looking back. Watching the dead match fall from her fingers, I remember the last day we were friends.

We were twelve. We were with two boys in the alley behind my house. Dee said, "C'mon, let's go in this garage." I said I didn't want to. She said, "Why not?"

"It's too dark in there," I said. "There isn't any light."

Dee pulled a book of matches from her pocket and held it up and said, "Here's some light."

"Those won't last long," I warned her. Behind her, a mulberry tree twisted upward from the dirt, dropping purple berries that splotched and stained the ground.

The boys were watching us, shy yet eager, waiting for whatever we'd toss their way.

"You're just scared," Dee said. "She's just scared," she said to the boys. "She wants to grow up to be an old maid."

"I do not," I said. I was planning on marrying and having three children, but I kept that to myself.

"See you later, Old Maid," Delia said, and she went into the garage with the boys following her. I walked out of the alley, listening to her laugh, wishing I could have what she had.

And as she drives away in her battered Jeep, I still want it. Her laugh. Those boys. Her nerve. The dark. I even want her baby bird, though I know that's a crazy thought. I even want her quiet son, even though I know I wouldn't be able to save us both.

Lorelei

In the mornings, I write stories; in the afternoons, I drive for the public bus that provides door-to-door service in and around Saugatuck, Michigan. We carry young and old, rich and poor, able-bodied and disabled: anyone who needs or wants a ride. How we drivers feel about our riders depends on the particular passenger and the driver, but almost all of us, including me, grumbled about picking up Lorelei. Her wheelchair was dirty, sticky to the touch on the handles and everywhere else. Bits of dried gunk were stuck to the frame, and strands of Lorelei's long, white hair had wound themselves around the joints above the casters. We couldn't help but brush up against some of this when we used the tie-downs to secure her wheelchair to the floor, and if Lorelei got up and moved to a bus seat, which she usually did—with such ease that we wondered why she bothered using a wheelchair—her butt sometimes made a wet imprint on the bus's upholstery.

Whenever I boarded Lorelei, I'd try to persuade her to stay in her wheelchair without telling her why. I'd say it made more sense for her to stay put since I had to strap down her chair whether she was in it or not. But as soon as I backed her and her wheelchair from the lift onto the bus, she'd get up and slip onto a seat, her face furtive and then stubborn as she avoided my eyes. Watching her, my own face would turn irritable and sour. After Lorelei disembarked, I'd check to see if the seat she'd sat on was wet; if it was, I'd tear paper towels from the roll and lay them on the damp spot so no one else would sit there.

Lorelei would ride every day for a month, then not at all for a few weeks. During a phase when she was riding daily, she kept remarking on a car parked on the Blue Star Highway just north of Saugatuck that had a for-sale sign taped to the window. Every time we passed it, she'd say in her Arkansas drawl, "I wish I knew how much that car cost. I've been looking to buy me a car."

One evening as I was driving in my own Honda Civic past the Buick Lorelei had her eye on, I turned in to the gravel lot, pulled up close to the Buick, and copied the phone number and asking price on a three-by-five card. My brother Arthur was with me. "I'm writing down these numbers for one of my passengers," I explained. "She's been talking about buying this car."

"Wow, Annie, that's so nice of you to do that for your passenger," Arthur said.

I gave him the same sour look that came over my face in Lorelei's presence. "I'm not doing it for my passenger."

"You're not?"

"No. I'm not doing it to be nice."

"Oh!" Arthur said. He laughed. "You're doing it to get her off your bus!"

⊙

At least part of my aversion toward Lorelei was rooted in my upbringing. Although my parents were politically progressive, I'd been raised with some prejudice. Not toward the usual targets—African Americans and Mexican Americans and other people of color—but against southern whites. My family lived in Detroit, but my dad had marched in Alabama and seen them up close, their faces contorted by rage. These were the people, he said, who attacked and killed an untold number of black southerners, as well as civil rights workers of both colors from the North and South, including the best and the brightest, Dr. Martin Luther King. My dad loathed Bull Connor, James Earl Ray, and the rest of those southern racists. He also thought northern rural whites were suspect. Once when I wanted to go camping by myself near Ortonville, a small town north of Detroit, my dad wouldn't let me for fear of the local "rednecks."

Of course, even urban whites from northern cities could be racist; my dad's own mother was a case in point—an Italian immigrant from Queens who disparaged her Puerto Rican neighbors. Once, when I was fifteen, I said to her, "Grandma, I can't always tell the difference between Puerto Ricans and Italians." This was the plain truth. What I said next, while also true, was sly; my intent was to needle her. "Like what about your friend Margie Tonelli?" I asked. "Are you sure she's Italian? She looks Puerto Rican to me."

Through clenched teeth, my grandma answered, "You can always tell Puerto Ricans from Italians because Italians are *clean!*"

But back to my father's prejudice, which became also my own: while we've never used the uglier slur "white trash," which seems a terrible phrase to use for a person, at times both of us have referred to rural white people as rednecks.

⊙

When I gave the card with the phone number and the Buick's price to Lorelei, she told me some involved story about having the money for the car but not being able to arrange for insurance right now. A few weeks passed. Someone else bought the car, and Lorelei continued riding the bus.

On the day before Thanksgiving, I picked up Lorelei from Christian Neighbors, a charity that distributes donated clothing and food. She was grumbling about something not being fair and the Mexicans and being cheated as I pushed her wheelchair onto the lift. A volunteer carried her bags of groceries up onto the bus and left without a word. After I'd strapped down Lorelei's chair and returned to my seat, she was still grumbling.

"What's not fair?" I asked her.

"They gave all the turkeys to the damn Mexicans, and all I got was a lousy chicken."

My back was to her, so she couldn't see my smile. "Well," I said, "they probably did that because there's only one of you, and the Mexicans have families."

Lorelei didn't respond.

"That makes sense, doesn't it?" I said. "To give bigger birds to families and smaller birds to single people?"

"I don't care," Lorelei said. "I wanted a turkey."

I drove up the Blue Star Highway and then made several turns, the last into the Ridgewood Oaks complex, where Lorelei lived. Remembering a previous conversation, I asked, "Aren't you going to your granddaughter's for Thanksgiving? Won't you get to eat some turkey there?"

"No, I won't," Lorelei said. "She's making a damn ham."

⊙

Shortly after Thanksgiving, each bus was equipped with a bottle of hand sanitizer, so after I'd touched Lorelei's sticky chair and she was off the bus, I'd squirt some onto my hands and wipe them clean with a paper towel. The weather was exceptionally mild for late November, and one day when Lorelei rode she made a remark about the crazy warm weather. I told her I was still picking lettuce and greens from my garden, and Lorelei said that her mother used to grow greens, and also watermelons and corn, back in Arkansas. She went on to tell me that her grandpa was a preacher, and they had to get dressed up every Sunday to hear him preach. "It was just a little bitty church," Lorelei said. "And so hot in the summer. You should have heard me complain. My daddy said hell fire would feel hotter, and that's where I was going."

"Do you go to church now?" I asked.

"No," Lorelei said. "I got in all my church time when I was little."

As fall became winter, my fellow drivers continued to complain about Lorelei's stained, soiled clothes and her grimy, sticky chair, which they still didn't like to touch, even though we now had sanitizer to clean up with after she rode. But at least Lorelei no longer smelled like urine, and the bus seats she sat on stayed dry. I mentioned this to Di, another driver, and Di said Lorelei had told her she was getting Depends from somewhere—her son or her daughter or maybe Christian Neighbors. "She can't afford them herself," Di said. "Those things are super expensive."

One day Lorelei told me she was going to buy some lottery tickets, and she hoped she'd win enough to pay off the three thousand dollars she owed in medical bills.

"Can't you get some help from Medicare for your bills?" I asked.

"They won't pay it because I have a certificate in the bank. They want me to give that up first, but I won't do it."

I tried to talk Lorelei out of her plan. "They say you're more likely to get struck by lightning than win the lottery," I said.

"Yeah, I heard that, too," she said. "But I'm going to buy me some anyway. I've won before. Though nothing to brag on."

Since the only thing Lorelei was buying at the store was the tickets and we weren't busy, I waited for her. When I'd got her back onto the bus and had punched her card, she said she'd spent her last forty dollars on scratch-offs. I kept quiet, wishing I'd said something more convincing than my lightning remark.

"If I win," Lorelei said, "I'll call you back in a bit for a ride to the store. I need to buy me some groceries."

She didn't call back that day.

⊙

A week later, as I was driving Lorelei home from the grocery store, she told me she'd been feeling sick all afternoon.

I said something commiserative but I was thinking, why don't people *stay home* when they're sick? Why do they have to ride the bus and expose everyone else to whatever they've got? Recently a passenger had taken her feverish first-grader all over town. As I was remembering this, I heard retching. I looked in the rearview. Lorelei was holding her grocery bag up to her mouth. I was relieved to see that she was vomiting into the bag rather than on the seat or the floor. She had removed from the bag the couple of items she'd bought—a box of chocolate-covered donuts and a pack of cigarettes—and set them beside her.

"Are you okay?" I asked.

"Yeah," she said, sounding dejected. "I'm sorry."

"Don't worry about it."

"I didn't think I'd be puking on the bus."

"It's no big deal," I said. "It's happened before."

"I knew I shouldn't have eaten that lunch meat," Lorelei said. She vomited into the bag again. "I'm so sorry," she repeated. It was the first time I'd heard Lorelei sound down-hearted and ashamed.

"Don't worry about it," I said again. "And thanks for using the bag. That saves me some trouble."

When we arrived at Ridgewood Oaks, I called in to the dispatcher that Lorelei was sick, and it was going to take me a little extra time to help her off the bus. Meanwhile, two regular passengers from the building next to Lorelei's were standing outside, ready to board: Bart, an alcoholic who was nearing the end of drinking himself to death, and Liv, who had some sort of mental disability but one that didn't seem too severe. I called to them, "Can one of you get me a plastic bag from your apartment? I need to double bag this"—I held up the bag of vomit—"before I put it in the dumpster." They shook their heads vigorously, eyes exaggeratedly wide—you'd think the bag was contaminated with Ebola and I'd asked them to dispose of it themselves. I sighed, walked down off the bus, knotted the bag, took it over to the empty dumpster, and dropped it in, wondering if it was too late to switch careers. I had an MFA in creative writing—maybe I'd published enough now to land a teaching job. The bag hit the metal bottom of the dumpster and jiggled but didn't break. But my hands were a little wet—some of the vomit had ended up on the outside of the bag. This bus was missing its bottle of sanitizer and was also out of paper towels, so I asked Lorelei if I could wash up in her apartment, and she said yes. I rolled her onto the lift, powered her down to the pavement, and pushed her chair through the double entrance doors of her building and then all the way into her apartment.

Lorelei apologized for the mess, but my overall impression as I glanced around, being careful not to stare, was that her apartment was not as bad as I'd thought it would be. "I'm getting ready to move, is why everything is kind of tore apart," Lorelei said.

"It doesn't look bad at all," I said. And it really didn't. The furniture seemed to be set in the right places, I didn't notice dirty dishes lying around, and the floor wasn't too cluttered.

I asked Lorelei if she wanted me to call someone for her.

"No," she said. "I'm just going to get out of these clothes and into the bathtub." I noticed then that the front of her blouse had a wet streak. "You go on and wash up first," she said, pointing me toward a door next to the kitchen.

The sink and toilet didn't look as dirty as my own sink and toilet sometimes did, which is not a testament to Lorelei's house-cleaning habits as much as a mark against my own—if I'd inherited any Italian cleanliness genes from my Grandma Zito, they apparently were recessive. I washed my hands and dried them on the thighs of my pants instead of the hanging towel, in case Lorelei was vomiting due to some intestinal bug. Then I returned to Lorelei and again asked if she wanted me to call anyone. I felt bad leaving her, sick and alone.

"No, I'll be all right," she said.

"You don't need your daughter or son to come over and help you?" I asked.

"No," she said. "I'll be fine."

I patted her shoulder and told her to take care. Then I went back out to my bus, where wide-eyed Bart and Liv were still waiting to board. After they were settled and I had driven off, I thought of my dad. He'd suffered from Parkinson's for over a decade, and in the past couple of years he had grown significantly worse. But unlike Lorelei, he received round-the-clock care, from my mom and home-care aides who cost far more than Lorelei could afford.

☉

After that day, Lorelei was less surly with me. I had softened toward her, too, and one day when I picked her up, I asked her how old she was. "Just turned eighty," she said proudly.

"You're the same age as my mom," I told her.

But my mom walked without a walker or even a cane, she did yoga almost every day, and she'd never smoked. She was perpetually exhausted from taking care of my dad, it was true, but if she deteriorated or faltered, she'd have all the health-care professionals she needed plus me and my four brothers and sister to rely on.

I knew that both Lorelei's son and her daughter lived in nearby towns, and as I drove, I asked Lorelei how often she saw them.

"Now and then," she said. "It depends."

"And besides your granddaughter in Fennville, do you have any other family close by?"

"No," she said. "My brothers and sisters are all back in Arkansas. But we don't get along. They didn't even call me when our ma died, so I missed the funeral."

"That's terrible," I said.

"Other than them, my only family was my husband—I used to be married, a real long time ago."

I had Johnny Cash on the CD player, turned down low, singing about someone's blue eyes he couldn't forget. Lorelei said, "One night my husband was walking home from the bar and he got runned over."

"Did he get badly hurt?" I asked.

"No," she said. "He got dead."

"Oh," I said. Her matter-of-fact tone stopped me from saying I was sorry.

"That was the best-est day of my life," Lorelei said.

I didn't know how to respond to that, so I stayed silent.

"He used to beat the crap out of me," Lorelei said. "That's why I took up smoking. I was so nervous, waiting for him to get home. I knew what was coming."

Her husband died when their children were young, Lorelei told me, so she got a series of factory jobs and raised her children without anyone's help. "I was a good-looking woman," Lorelei said. "I could have married again. But I wasn't taking no more chances."

I'd never considered whether Lorelei was good-looking or not—either currently or when she was younger. She did have pretty hair, long and white and still fairly thick, with a bit of a curl. And if I ignored her stained clothes and focused on her face, it was pleasant enough. As a young woman, she wouldn't have had the exaggerated bags under her eyes that she did now, or the sagging cheeks and wattled neck. Looking past the dirt and the years to her high cheekbones and wide blue eyes, I saw that she had likely been quite beautiful once.

⊙

Weeks passed, then months. Lorelei bought a car, and I only saw her if she happened to be outside when I was driving through Ridgewood Oaks to make another pickup or drop-off. Then one snowy day in early March, she was back on my bus. Car trouble, I guessed, but she said no, there was just too much snow on her car windows for her to wipe off. I took her to the store, and later I picked her back up. She wasn't in a wheelchair—she was using one of those walkers fronted by a large, flat shelf good for carrying groceries, handbags, and other items. A store employee helped carry Lorelei's groceries onto the bus and set the bags on the floor. He put a gallon jug of milk on the shelf of Lorelei's walker, but I didn't notice that at the time.

When I pulled into Ridgewood Oaks, even though I took the first, tight curve at only a few miles per hour, Lorelei's milk jug slid from her walker shelf and hit the floor. I turned around at the sound. Milk was leaking from the gallon jug. I shifted the bus into park, got out of my seat, walked back to the jug, and stood it up on the floor. Next I grabbed the roll of paper towels and mopped up the spilled milk. But the milk kept flowing; the side of the jug had split. I picked up the jug, walked with it down the steps of the bus, and set it on the snowy pavement.

I'd been told by the dispatcher to pick up a passenger at Building C, and red-haired Rochelle, who tends bar at the Cove, was outside waiting to board. "Want me to get a plastic bag to put that milk in?" she asked.

"That would be great," I said, and Rochelle hurried back into her building.

While I mopped up the rest of the milk, Lorelei apologized. "I should've known that jug wouldn't stay where he set it. Now I made a mess on your bus again." I told her not to worry; it was no big deal. I was happy to be dealing with good, clean milk rather than vomit, and grateful that Rochelle was helping to solve the problem.

Rochelle came back out with not one but *two* plastic bags, put the jug inside them, and handed the jug to me. "I noticed it's only split near the top," she said. "So it won't leak too much more." I thanked her and set the jug on the floor.

After returning to my seat, I pulled the bus around to Ridgewood G. As Lorelei rode down on the lift, holding the handles of her walker, she apologized again, and I assured her again that a little spilled milk wasn't a problem.

⊙

Later, another driver told me that Lorelei said I'd been so nice to her that day. I shook my head, smiling to myself and thinking: *vomit . . . spilled milk . . . what next?* I considered stopping at Lorelei's car and sweeping off the snow so she could drive it—and therefore not ride on my bus again right away—but we no longer kept brooms on our buses. And I had plenty of other things to attend to, at work and in my spare time, besides clearing the snow from Lorelei's car.

Still, I thought about Lorelei's situation, and I worried a little. It occurred to me that my dad would look like Lorelei did if he had no one to give him baths, wash his clothes, change his diapers, and dress him. Lorelei was more mobile and independent than my dad, but she obviously needed more help than she was getting. Once, stepping onto the lift with her walker, she sighed and said things were getting to be too much for her and she was thinking of moving into a nursing home. And so one day soon after that, when Lorelei rode again, I asked her if she had looked into any nursing homes and if she was still thinking of living in one.

"I was in one before, for a couple of weeks," she said. "But I didn't like it."

"Why? Didn't they feed you well?" I asked, my voice warm and kind—I'd grown fond of Lorelei. Between the vomit and the spilled milk, we had bonded. And although I didn't always approve of what she said, I liked that she spoke her mind.

"The food wasn't a problem," Lorelei said. "I didn't like the physical therapist."

Again my voice was kind, almost caressing, as I asked, "Did she work you too hard?"

"It wasn't a lady. It was a man." She paused. "And he was black."

I smiled and sighed to myself. My voice still sweet, though a little less gentle, I asked, "Was that a problem?"

Now Lorelei sighed, out loud. "I'm just not used to it, Annie," she said, with a note of pleading in her voice. "I'm from the South. We don't mix down there like you do up here."

I was trying to think of how to respond, so I didn't answer her right away.

"When I was growing up," Lorelei said, "we didn't have any blacks at all in our town. They weren't allowed to live there, and if they came around to fish, we'd shoot their boats out from under them."

I stifled a surprised cry. Then I pulled out of Ridgewood Oaks and cruised down Maple Street. I still hadn't thought of what to say to Lorelei.

"I'm just not used to being around black people," Lorelei said again.

I gathered my thoughts, even though I knew I wouldn't be able to speak succinctly and clearly about such a complex and charged subject. But finally, I gave it a try: "Where I grew up, in Detroit, there were a lot of black people," I said, "and they weren't too different from white people. Some were nice, and some were mean."

Lorelei was quiet. Then she said, "Well, where I'm from, the black men were always trying to get with the white women."

Again I searched for something to say that would make a difference. As I was trying to frame an answer, Lorelei said, "At least, that's what they told me."

Ah! I thought, happy that she doubted what she'd been told, that there was at least a crack I could work to widen.

"Well," I finally said, "some black men want to get with white women, and some white men want to get with black women." And then I rambled on about how there were all kinds of ways for black people to be, just like white people. I might have also said something Rodney King–like about how we should all try to get along.

Lorelei didn't respond right away, so I asked her what town in Arkansas she was from.

"Little Rock," she answered.

"Little Rock!" I exclaimed. "That's a big city! And Clinton's from there, and he gets along great with black people!"

"Oh, he gets along with anyone who will sleep with him," Lorelei said with a smile in her voice.

"He gets along with black men, too," I said, "and he doesn't sleep with them. Don't you know they call him the first black president?"

Lorelei laughed. "And I guess if his wife gets elected, she'll be the first black lady president."

We both laughed.

After a pause, Lorelei said, "I wouldn't have minded too much having a black therapist. Except that he was flirting with me."

I considered this possibility and dismissed it, if only because of the disparity there would have to be in their ages. I had pulled up to a stop sign. I turned around in my seat. "I bet he wasn't really flirting," I said. "I bet he was just trying to be friendly. Trying to get you to smile and be nice."

Lorelei laughed, and I saw what looked like delight in her eyes. Then she smiled down at her lap and said, "You might be right."

Over the next few months, Lorelei continued to ride my bus. I was always happy to see her. She still grumbled and complained, but I could tell she was pleased to see me, too. One Friday afternoon as we were saying good-bye, she said, "Next time I call in to the switchboard, I'm going to ask can *you* come to get me."

"You can try," I said. "Though it'll depend what else is going on—where the other drivers are, and where everybody has to go."

"All right, then," she said. "I'll ask for you and hope I get you."

Before I drove away, I happened to look at Lorelei again. She was staring off into space, and something about her eyes and the set of her face made me think of the word *regal*. As I continued to watch her, I noticed the deep lines crossing her cheeks. She looked dignified—and, yes, like some sort of queen. I knew she'd been beautiful once; now I realized she was beautiful still. I doubt it was the first time she'd looked that way. But it was the first time I saw it.

⊙

The following Monday, I pulled into the Ridgewood Oaks complex to drop a passenger and saw a cluster of emergency vehicles parked outside Lorelei's building. There were four of them: an ambulance, a fire truck, a police car, and a first-responder van. Immediately I thought of Lorelei. Then I thought of Ira, our other elderly passenger from Building G. I hoped both were all right. But all the emergency vehicles were silent, their flashers were off, and the two responders walking between them were moving slowly. There was, all too clearly, no need to hurry.

The next day, I learned Lorelei had died. I heard conflicting stories from my coworkers and her neighbors about what had happened and when: she'd had a heart attack; no, she had fallen and hit her head. She'd been found on Sunday by her son; actually, her body hadn't been discovered until Monday evening, which was when I'd seen the emergency vehicles gathered outside.

Over the next couple of weeks, I questioned my other passengers, but even those who lived in Lorelei's building didn't have more information about her. One of my coworkers and I searched the papers every day, and we looked up the local funeral homes online. I wanted to learn more about Lorelei: the names of her son and her daughter, how many sisters and brothers she had. I thought I would go to the visitation or the funeral. But we found no mention of her.

⊙

Months have passed since I last looked for Lorelei's obituary. But I still think of her when I pull my bus up to her building. A new passenger has moved into Lorelei's old apartment, and last night for the first time I carried in her groceries. I looked around as I set the bags down, as if I might somehow find a trace of Lorelei remaining. The apartment was crowded with furniture and knick-knacks. It looked wholly unfamiliar, and it also seemed smaller, as if the walls had shouldered in closer and the ceiling had dropped down. I felt a pang of regret and dismay, and a flutter of sadness. There was nothing of Lorelei left. I wanted to ask the new tenant, *Do you know anything about the woman who lived here before you?*

I wanted to say *Lorelei*. I wanted to hear someone speak her name.

⊙

Note
to the
New
Owners

Look for morels the first week in May, near the three white pines to the west of the house. Morels are supposed to grow near apples and oaks, but I never saw any until I planted these pines. Sometimes they've appeared right under the pine trio, pushing their way up like small ghosts through the brown, fallen needles.

Fronting the barn are gooseberry bushes. Pick their fruit for jam in mid-June, when they're light green like grapes, with just a few turning rosy.

Most of the pond will be gone by late fall, but don't worry—in spring, at its fullest, water will cover the roots of the willows.

Turn on the light in the pump box when the forecast calls for single digits. If you forget, and the pump freezes up, don't panic! Set a small space heater in the box, and the frozen water will quickly thaw.

I hope you enjoy your new home!

If you don't like morels, or want to sell some, let me know.

⊙

My mom started this note, and then she put it in the recycling, but I took it out and up to my room so I could finish it and leave it on the kitchen counter for you.

I'm eleven and the daughter of the house. I make dolls out of cloth. My best doll is Josephine. I am taking her with me. I'm leaving Esmeralda for you, and also so she can watch over the house. Please take care of her. She likes to sit in the deep nook above my chimney.

This house has lots of great nooks and crannies, but mice live on the other side of the miniature door that leads to the other attic. Just open it once, so you can see what's over there: boards slanting up, holding the roof, and lots of insulation and dust and tiny mouse turds. Then latch that door and leave it closed, and try not to think about how it's dark there and dirty and mice run loose all over. Stick to the finished part of the attic, where I lived, under the slanty roof. It's so cold in winter I had two goose-down quilts covering me and so hot in summer I kept the fan running all day and all night. But it's the best room in the house, with four windows and a pine floor with a braided rug made by my mom.

I'm taking the rug to my new bedroom, which is a totally boring box on the first floor. We're moving in with my mom's friend. I'm not sure that's the greatest idea. I've lived with my dad part of the time ever since I was six, but my mom is used to living with no one but me.

We're leaving here because my mom got sick of spiders spinning webs in every corner, poison ivy creeping up onto the deck, coyotes howling and yipping in the yard, raccoons pressing their faces to the screens on the porch. Also groundhogs chewing on the foundation and burrowing into the crawlspace, and don't forget the neighbor boys climbing up onto the roof and trying to take the cover off the chimney—don't ask me what for. We're moving onto a real street in Royal Oak, which is just north of Detroit. My mom says we're moving back into civilization.

I will miss the country. The owls calling at night and the coyotes, too, the tree frogs trilling like birds, all the night insects at the end of the summer, like tonight, right now. My mom says she'll miss the morels that show up every spring just in time for Mother's Day and the sandhill cranes flying overhead in the fall like pterodactyls. And she'll miss the three pines she planted for my sister, who died when she was just a baby. My mom says she'll plant a new grove at the new house, in the backyard, but they can't be like these pines are right now, so big that birds have built nests in their branches, and you can climb them if you're light like me and look inside to see the eggs.

Once, back by our pond, we saw something really sad but also kind of cool: a frog whose belly got bit by the smallest snapping turtle you ever saw. The turtle hung on, and the frog kicked and kicked, trying to swim away from the turtle's clamped mouth, but the turtle wouldn't let go. Finally, the frog gave one last kick and tore away from the turtle, tearing open its own belly, spilling a stream of frog guts behind it in the water as it glided. We knew the frog would die. My mom said it was a lesson in biology and survival and I tried not to cry. That night after supper, I picked black-eyed Susans for the frog and laid them under the pines.

At our new house, there's a lawn and hardly any trees and no turtles or frogs or pond. But summer insects live there, too, and cardinals and chickadees, and of course there are squirrels. I don't think there are raccoons. But maybe one will follow us from our old house and climb up onto our new porch, press its face to the screen, and look inside.

⊙

My mom says she thinks the new owners of our old house are young, because of your names, Emily and Aaron. She doesn't know if you have children, but I just want to say this is a perfect place for kids, and don't be afraid that your baby will die. My mom's first kid did. But then she had me, her second one, and I lived.

Unblinking

When Ralph wakes from his nap, he and Rosie play chess. Rosie sets up the board and the pieces, Ralph helping as much as he can. Then they hunker over the game—silent, intent—and before long Ralph is up by a pawn and a knight. That's the strange thing about the dementia caused by his Parkinson's—it's left parts of his brain untouched. And it comes and goes without warning. Ralph can be coherent and lucid one minute, beating her at chess, and the next he's off in a different world, one where Rosie isn't able to follow. Lately, Ralph's been seeing his only brother, four years younger, who died of a heart attack twenty-two years ago. Ralph will look up at the empty air, break into a happy grin, and call out, *"Johnny!"* as if Johnny has just walked into the room. Ralph was raised Catholic, but he turned away from religion in his teens, drawn toward the science that would lead him to medical school. He doesn't believe in angels or ghosts, yet now he is seeing them.

Rosie concedes the first game, Ralph the second one. They rarely play to the bitter end. When it becomes clear that the other will win, the loser gives in.

Rosie remembers the games they played when they were younger. Then, the loser was often angry, the winner teasing, even gloating. If Rosie lost, she would bite her lip and go silent. Ralph, grinning, would say in a sugary voice, "What's the matter, babe?"

"Oh shut up," she would answer.

"What? You're mad? What are you mad about?" Ralph would ask, as if astonished, enjoying her quiet anger, trying to draw it out.

"I shouldn't have let you take that move back."

"Well, why did you then?"

"Because you insisted!"

"You could have said no! Don't lay it on me, babe." He'd still be grinning.

She would abruptly push back the table and stand up.

"Aw, don't be mad," Ralph would tease.

"I'm not mad. I'm just never playing with you again, that's all."

And Ralph would laugh with delight, throwing his head back. (Something he can't do anymore; he can barely turn his neck.)

But Rosie had enjoyed teasing him just as much—ten, twenty, fifty years ago. Back then, when Ralph realized he'd lost a game, he wouldn't say, "I resign"—instead he'd start snatching up the pieces and tossing them roughly into the box. Or he'd upend the board, sending the kings and queens flying, scattering across table and floor.

Rosie would smile as broadly as was possible while still keeping her mouth closed. "Ralphy," she'd say sweetly, knowing he didn't want sweetness right then, that her pleasure was an irritant, "it's just a game. Somebody has to lose."

"You didn't beat me," he'd say.

"Oh, really?"

"Yes. I beat myself."

"Oh," she would say, "so when *you* win, *you* beat *me*, but when *I* win, you beat yourself?"

"That's right. I played a lousy game. I gave that game to you."

She'd continue to smile. Then she'd say, "Want to play another?"

"No."

"Oh, c'mon. Don't you want another chance to beat yourself?"

"Go to hell."

"Oh, Ralphy," she'd say, laughing, with love in her voice.

"Kiss my ass," he'd say. But his anger never lasted. Sometimes he would start setting up the pieces again in the midst of his swearing.

These days their games are far quieter. Ralph hunches over the board, silent, his large eyes unblinking, his face resembling a mask. But he can still beat her about half the time. Occasionally, if she wins two games in a row, she'll back off and let him win the third. She doesn't really mind if she loses. Chess isn't even her favorite game; she prefers Scrabble. But Ralph hates the Scrabble dictionary with all of its "bullshit words," and he thinks it's ridiculous that you can end up with all vowels or all consonants or all one-point letters. So she plays

Scrabble with three of her women friends, all four of them retired math teachers from Mumford High. They started out playing biweekly, but as they've grown older, they've scaled back to once a month. It's the opposite with chess. As Ralph's illness worsens, Rosie plays chess with him more and more often. Ralph can no longer read a book, swim a lap, or walk without a walker. Chess is one of his few pleasures that has not yet been subtracted, so he and Rosie play every day that they can.

This afternoon, after each wins one game, Rosie starts putting the pieces away, and Ralph joins in; his hands tremble and he has trouble closing his fingers, but he grips the rooks and bishops, lifts them, and drops them into the box.

Today Rosie's fingers and brain are also clumsier and slower. She is more tired than usual because the day before yesterday, she fired Angels in the Home. The owners of Angels told her she had to start paying a higher rate because Ralph had become harder to care for, and that rubbed Rosie the wrong way. Did they expect things would get *better*? He has Parkinson's! Do they know what the word *degenerative* means? Well, it was a relief, anyway, to no longer have strangers in their apartment all day and night, different ones all the time, some more helpful than others. Most of the aides were very nice, but they don't need the extra hassle or the expense. Rosie can help Ralph stand up and transfer from chair to wheelchair or wheelchair to bed without anyone's assistance but his—at least for now, until he gets worse. If he tries to walk without his walker and makes a misstep and falls, she can call the downstairs desk, and they'll send someone from security or maintenance to lift Ralph back up. Rosie can help him onto and off of the shower chair, and she can roll him on the bed and change his diapers by herself. The last aide bought the wrong size—large, when medium is what fits. She remembers this as they are putting away the chess pieces. "Oh, Ralphy, I forgot we were going to go to the store today for more briefs." She looks out the windows. The sky, blue all morning, is now a light gray.

"What time is it?" Ralph asks.

"A little after four. We can still make it, I think."

The part of downtown Detroit where they live is really quite safe, but only in the daytime is it *surely* safe. At night, or even at dusk, they are taking their chances going out. About a year ago, one of their older friends was mugged a half mile east of here. And last month shots were fired in the dollar store next to the Lafayette Market, the grocery down the street where they shop. Luckily no one was hit by a bullet or even robbed: an employee tripped an alarm, and the would-be robber took off. But then two weeks ago, right at dusk, Fred Munson, who lives in their building, was shot in the stomach by a young man who demanded the keys to his car. The bullet passed through Fred without hitting anything vital, and even though he is seventy-nine, he came home from the hospital after only a week. But he still has a long way to go until he is fully recovered.

Rosie hasn't yet told any of their kids about Fred being shot only one short block from their apartment, in the parking lot of the liquor store where she occasionally picks up a bottle of Canadian Club. She's afraid they will insist that she and Ralph move somewhere safer, even though their son Zachary, who is a nurse, has said that when people as ill and elderly as Ralph are moved out of their homes, they usually go into a rapid decline and quickly die. That's reason enough to stay in their apartment, where they've lived for twenty-seven years. But they also simply like it here. She and Ralph still enjoy strolling and wheeling along the Riverwalk, through the park right next to their condo, and down the aisles of the Eastern Market on Saturday mornings, pushing through the crowds with their bags of produce hanging from the handles of Ralph's chair. And if they left Detroit, they would miss their friends who live in their condo, plus those few others who haven't died or moved out of the area and who still stop by to visit. Ralph has never wanted to live where the majority of people are white and Republican and many are bigots, and while Rosie doesn't phrase it exactly like that, she feels the same.

"Let's go, Rosie," Ralph says, his voice loud and forceful—sometimes his voice is as strong and unaffected as it was before Parkinson's. "We'll have enough time if we leave right away."

But there's no such thing as "right away" anymore, especially when it comes to getting out of the house. First, Ralph has to use the bathroom—the diapers are only for backup; he hates to pee in his pants and then sit in his own piss—and that takes a while. Then Rosie puts on Ralph's shoes and works his down coat onto him. Finally she gets on her own coat and shoes and finds her keys and her change purse.

Rosie could run this errand more quickly on her own, but she doesn't like leaving Ralph alone—sometimes he gets confused about how long she's been gone and goes looking for her. After coming home twice to find him helpless on the floor, Rosie decided it was no longer safe to leave him behind. And

Ralph doesn't like her going to the store by herself, anyway. Ralph still considers himself Rosie's protector, though any potential mugger can see that he's no longer strong enough to defend even himself. He thinks she is safer in his company, as if his mere presence or his will alone can keep her from harm. And she does feel more secure when the two of them go out together, even though Ralph's strength is greatly diminished, as is her own, now that she's eighty-one, has arthritis in her hands, and has shrunk several inches, to five feet three.

Rosie locks their door behind them and wheels Ralph's chair to the elevators. One arrives quickly; she backs him into it, and they descend the six floors. But pushing him from the bank of elevators to the lobby seems harder than usual, as if something is wrong with the chair. She keeps going, though, until Ralph loudly calls, "Damn it, Rosie, stop!"

She stops pushing. "What's wrong?"

"We forgot to put on my footrests."

"Oh, shit," Rosie says. "We better go back and get them."

"No, it'll get too late," Ralph says. "We can manage without them."

"Are you sure?"

"Yeah. I can lift my feet and walk them as you push."

This works fairly well on the tiled floor near the elevators and in the lobby. As they pass the front desk, Itembe, the newest security employee, rises to open the doors for them. Rosie and Ralph thank him, and he wishes them a good evening. Pausing outside the apartment entrance, Rosie notes that the sky has grown slightly grayer. She considers driving to the store. Their car wouldn't appeal to a carjacker—it's a Honda Civic, six years old. Fred Munson had been driving his brand-new Lincoln Continental when he was shot. But it's become more and more difficult for Ralph to transfer onto a car seat, even with her help. It is easier to simply walk.

Rosie wheels Ralph through the main entry area onto the condo's circular drive and from there down to the sidewalk. Ralph helps by lifting his feet and "walking" them in front of the chair. It's awkward, even though Ralph is doing a good job of shuffling his feet. Rosie wishes they'd gone back for the footrests.

The concrete outside their building entrance is smooth and well maintained, but once they are on the public sidewalk, the going is rougher; some of the square, concrete slabs are tilted at slight angles, with short, weedy growth filling in the cracks where two slabs fail to meet. They've gone less than thirty yards when Rosie realizes that Ralph is slipping out of his chair. His missing footrests not only provide a shelf on which to prop his feet, they also help to hold the rest of his body in place. She stops the chair and manages to lift him up a little, but soon after she resumes pushing, he starts sliding back down, his nylon-covered down coat slipping against the chair's vinyl. When Rosie stops to pull him upright again, Ralph says, "I think you better just push. We'll never get there if we keep stopping." So she does.

But halfway down the long block, she sees what a bad idea this is—all the little jolts from rolling over the irregular pavement have caused Ralph's butt to slide to the edge of the seat. His head has slipped to the edge of the seatback, and his legs are sticking out at odd angles in front of the chair. "Can you scoot up a little?" Rosie asks.

"Are you kidding? Look at me. I can't move at all."

It's as if he has no muscles or bones, as if he is a bag of sand that has slipped down and halfway out of the chair. His neck is pressed against the top edge of the seatback—only his head, hanging out over the back of the chair, prevents him from slipping down further. Without a strong upward boost, he is eventually going to slip further forward and down until finally he falls onto the sidewalk.

Rosie locks the brakes and tries to pull Ralph up to a sitting position. She can't budge him a fraction. If she tries to back up, Ralph will slip off the seat onto the pavement. He might hit his head or wrench his back. And she's forgotten his hat, which would have protected him at least a little if his head struck the concrete. They should have gone back for the footrests! She looks back at their apartment building—it's too far away to call to or run to for help. Like she could run, anyway. She can't even walk briskly anymore.

She looks up the street. It's empty except for a slow-moving older black man coming their way, his head bare despite the cold, wearing a worn jacket and baggy pants that are slipped too far down, not in the style that young people affect, but like Ralph's pants slip accidentally at times—Rosie is always pulling them back up. As the man draws closer, Rosie sees that he is only around fifty and that he is obviously homeless. But he seems alert and steady enough on his feet to help them, so she calls to him: "Sir?"

The homeless man slows his steps even more.

"Sir," Rosie says again, "can you help us, please? My husband is slipping out of his chair."

The man's gaze runs over them. He seems uncertain or puzzled. "Want me . . . want me to call 911?" he asks. He reaches into one of his baggy pockets and pulls out an older-model cell phone.

"Oh, no, we don't need an ambulance," Rosie says. "He's not hurt, he's just slipped down too far, and I'm not strong enough to get him back up on my own. But if you take one arm, and I take the other, we can pull him upright again." Rosie wants to suggest that the man hitch up his own pants first—she is afraid they might slip down further as he pulls up on Ralph, and then she'll have two men all twisted up in their clothes. But she keeps quiet, and the homeless man steps in close, releasing a smoky, acrid smell from his jacket as he pulls up on one side and Rosie pulls up on the other.

They manage to get Ralph upright and his butt replanted near the inside edge of the seat. "There you go," the man says. "You all right now?" he asks Ralph.

"I'm fine now," Ralph says. "Thanks very much for your kindness."

"That's all right, Pops," the homeless man says. "But can I ask you a favor? I need five dollars to get me something to eat."

Rosie reaches into her pocket and pulls out her change purse, in which she carries not only change but also bills and her credit card. She unzips the purse and finds a ten, which she holds out to the man.

"God bless you and keep you safe," the man says, slipping the bill into his pants pocket. Then he turns away and continues down the street, walking more swiftly.

Rosie returns the change purse to her pocket and her attention to Ralph. They need to get going and get back home before dark. She grips the wheelchair's handles and resumes pushing. "Ralphy," she says, "try to hold yourself up straight."

"What the fuck do you think I'm doing?" Ralph says. "I'm not *trying* to fall." Rosie sighs but otherwise wheels him in silence, easing him carefully over the bumps of the slanted walk. Then Ralph asks, "Where's Mike?"

"Mike?" Rosie says. "He's in Nebraska."

"He was here a minute ago," Ralph says, seeming surprised that Mike, their oldest son, is gone.

"That wasn't Mike, that's just some man we don't know who stopped to help us."

"I know that," Ralph says. "Mike was standing behind him, off to the side. I wonder why he didn't come closer."

"Michael's in Nebraska," Rosie says. "He was here visiting us two weeks ago, remember?"

"He was here just a minute ago, too," Ralph insists. "Standing a few feet off. Or, if it wasn't Mike, it was someone who looked a lot like him."

"Oh," Rosie says. She wonders if Ralph is seeing his dead relatives again. She hopes he won't have any difficult or disturbing hallucinations until they are safely home. Sometimes at night he becomes argumentative and insistent—he'll say he needs to get up to go to a family member's wedding or a funeral, and Rosie is almost unable to keep him in their bed.

Ralph is slipping down in his chair again. Rosie stops, pulls him up a couple of inches, then resumes pushing. The sky is turning a purplish gray. It's right around dusk. They will never make it home before dark. But at least they reach the little strip mall and then the grocery store, which is at the mall's far end, without Ralph slipping down too far.

Outside the Lafayette Market, a private security guard is sitting in his car. The owners of the market hired Eagle

Security Services after those shots were fired in the adjoining dollar store. Rosie wonders if the liquor store where the carjacking happened hired any security afterward. She hasn't been back since Fred Munson was shot. If she shops there again, she won't walk or drive there at dusk or after dark. Poor Fred! How terrible to be shot, to have a bullet rip through your belly. But it could have been much worse. After the first shot, the man aimed the gun at Fred's face. A woman in the parking lot screamed, "Don't shoot him again, please don't shoot him again!" Fred threw his keys to the ground, and the carjacker scooped them up and drove off.

The market is active with people shopping, yet not crowded. Rosie doesn't stop for a cart but wheels Ralph straight to the toilet paper aisle, which is where this store keeps the adult diapers. Rosie lifts a square package of the correct briefs, which are bulky yet light, and Ralph accepts them onto his lap.

Retracing their path up the paper goods aisle, they pass a teenaged girl with braided and beaded hair wearing a sweatshirt on which is stamped in huge letters: CALL YOUR MOTHER. It reminds Rosie of the shirt on which her daughter Annie embroidered LOVE YOUR MOTHER in a semicircle around an image of the lovely green and blue Earth as seen from outer space. Thinking of that shirt reminds Rosie of how her and Ralph's world has shrunk. Currently, it includes only a couple square miles of Detroit. Soon it will likely shrink to within the walls of their apartment. She misses the things they used to enjoy—dinners out, ball games, concerts, plays. And trips across the country to visit their kids. But she doesn't want to go anywhere if Ralph can't go with her. Their goal now is to stay at home, for Ralph to live out the rest of his life in their apartment. They should be able to make that happen as long as Ralph doesn't hit his head or break a bone and wind up in the hospital. Or if his mind doesn't deteriorate to the point where she can no longer keep him safe.

Rosie chooses the shortest and, she hopes, the fastest checkout line, stopping behind a black man in his sixties with a pencil mustache. The man's hands rest on his cart, inside which is a green pepper, several cans of pinto beans, a package of sausages, a bottle of red wine, and a carton of grapefruit juice. The mustachioed man is dressed in tasteful, casual clothes in muted browns and grays, set off by a jazzy pink shirt. Standing ahead of him is a very tall, very dark-skinned man in his forties wearing a light blue dress shirt and a lavender tie. He is holding a can of tuna in one hand and his wallet in the other. Rosie is relieved when the cashier places the can inside a grocery bag. Now, after the man leaves the store, no one will see the tuna can glinting in his hand and possibly mistake it for a gun and shoot him.

When it's her turn, Rosie pays with cash. On the way out, she stops at the ATM and withdraws another two hundred dollars, since sometimes the machine in their building is out of order. With Ralph holding the big square bag of diapers on his lap, she wheels him out of the store, past the stone-faced security guard, who does not meet her eyes, and down the long stretch of sidewalk that borders the parking lot, stopping only once to pull Ralph up straighter.

It is night now—it gets dark so early, so quickly, this time of year! Beyond the parking lot, the sidewalk is less well lit, but all of the streetlights are working and Rosie can even make out the shadowy shapes of the trees in the park across the street where she and Ralph sometimes go for a stroll in the daytime.

She is wheeling Ralph across the street, using the crosswalk that young children use in the daytime for school, when she sees, off to the left, a group of four boys or young men in the distance, heading their way. The four don't veer into the park, but stay on the bordering sidewalk that will lead them to her and Ralph. They are swaggering, not in a threatening way, but as young men or teenagers tend to do, just as they swaggered down the halls at Mumford High.

Rosie had liked to say, when people asked if Mumford was all black, "No. We have one Indian boy." After the Indian boy graduated, the school was one hundred percent black, not counting the teachers, about a third of whom were white. Eddie Murphy had graduated from Mumford, and also Susan from Sesame Street. It was a middle-class school, and most of the kids were well behaved. But still, there was violence, at times fatal. One of Rosie's former students was killed the summer before she was to start college. She'd gone with her boyfriend to a house in her neighborhood, where they'd been told there was a party. But it turned out to be the wrong house. Inside was a drug dealer who didn't recognize the young couple on his steps, and he answered their knock with gunfire. The girl died right there, on the front porch. A bright and cheerful student, accepted to U of M, a future teacher, perhaps, maybe also a wife and mother someday.

Rosie pushes Ralph and his chair over the rough, slanted sidewalk. It is fully night now. But that doesn't mean they are in danger, even with four black teenaged boys walking behind them, who will certainly catch up to them, since she and Ralph can't help but move slowly. She shouldn't be afraid. The boys have as much right to be outside now as she and Ralph, and likely as much purpose. They could be walking to Greektown for pizza, or maybe just rambling around, like young people do. But she is afraid, and she feels bad for being more afraid than she would be if the boys behind her were white. She remembers a comedian she and Ralph saw twenty or more years ago at a comedy club on Jefferson, a few blocks from here. A young, black comedian with a round, expressive face, he told about how he was walking down the street one night when a car with two white couples pulled up and stopped at the red light, and how he heard *thunk-thunk-thunk-thunk*— four door locks being pushed down. The comedian had looked all around him on the stage, mimicking his fright on that night: where is the danger these white people have seen that he hasn't yet? He approaches the car, calling out, "Where is it? Where's the bad guy, where's the monster? Let me in the car with you! Don't leave me out here to get killed!" And then, seeing the fear in their eyes increase as they stare goggle-eyed at him, he realizes what they are so frightened of: "Oh—it's *me*. They're locking their doors against *me*." She and Ralph had laughed helplessly along with the rest of the audience, which was integrated.

Integrated—you never hear that word anymore; it died with Martin Luther King. She remembers the young Freedom Riders from Mississippi who stayed at their house when they rode the buses north to Detroit. She remembers Ralph leaving her and the kids for five days to march from Selma to Montgomery, and before that, she and Ralph and the kids going to hear Dr. King's first "I Have a Dream" speech, right here in

Detroit, walking from First Unitarian Church to downtown, pushing Danny, who was then their youngest, in his stroller. She was pregnant with Zachary, but she didn't know it yet. Now Zacky is fifty-one, or is he fifty-two? She is doing the math when Ralph's wheelchair lurches—she's hit a bump in the dark—and he slides from his chair to the concrete.

"Oh, Ralphy!" she cries. "I'm so sorry—are you okay?"

Ralph lets out a soft stream of curses. Rosie locks the wheelchair's brakes and bends over him. He is lying on his back inside his slippery down coat, his large eyes open. "I'm fine," he says calmly. "I didn't fall hard."

Rosie laughs with relief. "You are getting to be an expert at falling!" she teases. But she immediately sobers. How is she going to get him back up into his chair? But she already knows—she will have to ask the four teenagers for help. She glances behind her. They are less than half a block away, walking slowly toward them. One is wearing a hooded sweatshirt, one a down parka, and two have on only light jackets. As they draw closer, Rosie sees that one of the jacketed boys is walking a dog, a muscular brown dog with short hair and a snub nose, of that breed used for fighting.

Rosie draws in her breath. Ralph is lying on the ground like a piece of meat, like the dead deer they saw years ago at the edge of the woods on Belle Isle. She will kick the dog with all her might if it advances toward Ralph.

The four boys draw to a stop, less than fifteen feet off. They are the age of the boys she used to teach, boys who thought they were men. They had wanted to be called men, and Rosie had obliged them, aware that black men of all ages have long been called "boy" as an insult, and that children of all colors want to seem older than they are. But in her head, she still thought of her teenaged students as children. And now that she's past eighty, these four boys look younger than ever.

The boys are speaking to one another. Then they all laugh. Rosie thinks she hears derision in their tone. "Can you please help me lift my husband back onto his chair?" she calls, raising her voice over theirs, as she had done many times from the front of her classroom. "I hit a bump in the sidewalk and he slid out onto the ground." She thinks of what they must look like—two old, frail, white-haired white people on a broken sidewalk by a deserted park in downtown Detroit, one lying on his back, the other standing helplessly over him.

The boys shuffle closer. "Johnny!" Ralph calls, looking up.

A couple of the boys laugh again, and Rosie is afraid she hears an unkind note in their laughter. "Name's not Johnny, it's Lenny," the closest one says. He is bareheaded and tall, wearing a gold-colored windbreaker.

"Sorry I missed your funeral," Ralph says, and some of the boys laugh again. Ralph is not looking at Lenny, Rosie knows, but beyond him, at the sky.

At least one of the boys figures this out, too: "Old motherfucker seeing ghosts," the one wearing the parka says.

"Man, watch your motherfucking language," the boy holding the dog says. The dog whines and strains forward, toward Ralph. Rosie mentally readies herself to step between Ralph and the dog, Ralph and the boys. The boy jerks the dog's chain back hard, and the dog makes a choking, coughing sound like Ralph does when food gets caught in his throat, and sits back on its haunches.

But Ralph is oblivious—to the dog, to the boys, even to her. "Wanna play ball?" he asks, looking over Lenny's shoulder.

"With you, Gramps?" the boy in the hooded sweatshirt says. "You got a hoop in your yard?" More laughter travels among them.

"We gonna go one-on-one?" the boy wearing the parka says. "Or are you gonna take us all at once?"

"We can play for whatever you got in your wallet," the hooded boy says, and Rosie isn't sure if he is entirely joking. The lettering on the front of his sweatshirt is so faded and stripped off that Rosie wouldn't be able to read it even if the light were better. She will step between these boys and Ralph if they take one more swaggering step forward. She'd done it before, in her classroom—she'd stepped between boys facing off for a fight at least a half dozen times. She'd even stepped between two of them once after they'd thrown the first punches. Astonished, they had paused, and she had taken advantage of their surprise to speak. "I do not allow fighting in my classroom," she had said. The taller of those boys had looked down at her and said, "Lady, you must be crazy." But he'd turned away and walked out of her classroom, and she'd picked up a piece of chalk and resumed writing equations on the board.

Some of the children in that class would go on to hold down good factory jobs or become teachers, musicians, doctors, or engineers. Others would work in low-wage service jobs or be chronically unemployed. They would go to prison or die young. They would become drug addicts and dope pushers, alcoholics and other sorts of beaten-down men and women.

She looks at these four boys standing before her and over Ralph, unable to think of what to say to them, and feels a terrible dread. She will gladly give them her whole money-packed little purse to save Ralph. But what if money isn't enough? She doesn't know what she will do if she is robbed of the last months or years of Ralph's life. Suddenly she feels like a widow—she sees that empty space waiting for her, just up ahead. She feels like she did when Zachary was a toddler and he went missing for an hour and she feared he was dead. She feels like she did after Danny, at nineteen, fell into the cardboard box crusher at work, and the doctor slapped X-rays of his legs up on a lighted screen and said he would lose one leg for sure and probably both.

"God damn it, don't swing so hard!" Ralph says. He is still stretched out on his back and looking up at the sky. "Give it a good smack, don't club it to death!"

The boys laugh again. Rosie looks first at Lenny, then at the hooded boy. "My husband is seriously ill," she says, trying to keep her voice from quavering. "Can you please help him up? If it were your grandfather . . ."

The two boys exchange glances. Then Lenny gives a command, and all four of them surge forward. Rosie can't seem to step toward Ralph or lift a hand. The boys and the dog are all tangled up with Ralph, while she stands helplessly watching.

Ralph rises from their midst, jerkily but swiftly, and then he is in his chair again, upright and seemingly unharmed, with the four boys standing around him. The hooded boy is looking off toward the street, and the boy holding the leash has his head bent toward his dog. The boy in the parka nudges the broken sidewalk with his shoe. Lenny, whose gaze is flitting, flashes Rosie a slight smile.

Rosie is struck silent. Then Ralph calls her name.

She steps closer to him and asks, "What is it, Ralph?"

Ralph is gazing up from his wheelchair and swiveling his head, what little he can, trying to take in all four of the boys. "Why are all these people standing around?" he asks.

"They saw you fall out of your chair," Rosie explains, "and they helped you back up."

"They did?" Ralph says. He looks at the boys and sighs. "Thank you. Very much."

"That's all right," Lenny says. He pulls at the sleeves of his gold windbreaker, straightening the cuffs over his wrists. Then he asks, "What are y'all doing out here at night?"

Rosie remembers the diapers. "Oh," she says. "My husband's briefs . . . we came from the store . . . he dropped them when he fell."

"Briefs?" Lenny asks, his quick face puzzled.

"Diapers for adults," Rosie says. She looks around until she spots the pale package, off to the side on the grass.

Lenny turns to the other boys and says something.

"I ain't carrying no old dude diapers," the boy in the parka grumbles. But the hooded boy steps over to the bag of briefs, snatches it up, and carries it to Rosie.

Rosie thanks him and sets the bag on Ralph's lap. Then she looks from the sweatshirted boy to Lenny. "You've already helped us enormously," she says. "But . . . do you think . . . could you please . . . walk us back to our apartment? I'm afraid my husband will slip out of his chair again."

Lenny squints as if surprised. Then he asks, "Where y'all live?"

"Right down this street," Rosie says. "In that tall building past the park."

Lenny glances around at his friends. The sweatshirted boy shrugs. The boy holding the dog seems to nod. Lenny steps closer, to one side of Ralph's chair.

They start walking, Lenny on one side of Ralph and the boy with the dog on his other, Rosie pushing Ralph's chair, the other boys lagging behind. Lenny is holding onto Ralph's coat at his shoulder and saying something to Ralph about his brother—he was shot in the spine a year ago, Lenny says; he has to use a wheelchair to get around.

Rosie wonders if Ralph will mention their son Danny, in his fifties now, who has used a wheelchair ever since he lost his legs at nineteen, who has grown so swift and graceful in his chair that he plays basketball and even dances. But Ralph does not.

Ralph says to Lenny, "I'm so sorry about your brother," and Rosie glances up at the sky, where Ralph has seen his own brother this evening. She doesn't expect to see Johnny's ghost up there, and she doesn't, not even a trace. Yet it seems as if the sky overhead has grown deeper, and that the ground under her feet has expanded and is still spreading outward, connecting her to the rest of the Earth. In her mind, she sees what looks like light flowing over the ground through the city, and then traveling out over the rest of the country, following the arc of the Earth. She sees this bright current joining her to the world. Then her thoughts return to Ralph and the four boys and the dog, who is panting in the quiet and measuredly setting his feet—Rosie hears his nails clicking and scraping on the sidewalk.

Rosie continues to step, pushing Ralph. Lenny adjusts his grip on Ralph's coat to keep him from slipping, and Rosie leans her head over Ralph's other shoulder. "Ralphy, how are you doing?" she asks.

"I'm all right, Rosie," Ralph says.

Rosie smells the soap she used to shave Ralph this morning. She feels heat rising from the neck of his coat. All through the years, she has loved being near his warmth. She looks up at the darkened sky, hoping they will manage and even savor whatever time Ralph has left, and as she does her gaze is caught by the moon: a bright sliver, thin as the edge of a fingernail, curving around a dark globe that's almost lost in the surrounding blackness. She leans in again toward Ralph. "I don't know if you can see it," she says, "but there's a crescent moon up ahead. Above the buildings."

Ralph shifts his head backward, and his large eyes turn upward.

The boy walking the dog points with his free hand. "It's right up there," he says.

Ralph stares, unblinking, into the night sky. "I can see it," he says. "So delicate."

"Look how the clouds are moving across it," Rosie says. "It's gorgeous, isn't it?"

Marching

The train rocks and sways, taking me home to Detroit. We race along the edges of harvested fields, snow flying up from the tracks and creating a fine, white blur. We skirt small cities, the backsides of towns and people's backyards. We pass water towers, a power plant, graffiti on bridges in Battle Creek. Then we're in the countryside again, and I'm staring out at monotonous fields and bare scrub when a small scene grips my heart: a creek winding through a clearing enclosed by a stand of snow-covered trees. It's unassuming yet lovely, and even after the train has rattled past, I'm enthralled as well as saddened by that fleeting moment of beauty.

My sister picks me up at the train station, drives me downtown, and hugs me good-bye at the apartment entrance—she doesn't have time to come up. Laura, the doorwoman who lets me in, asks if Nichole is my sister and if she is the baby of the family. Yes and yes, I say. Nichole, eighteen years younger than I am, is the daughter of my father's ex-mistress. Our dad revealed and then introduced Nichole to our mom when Nicki was two, and then to my four brothers and me when Nicki was six. My dad's affair caused my parents a lot of strife, but since then—for the past thirty-seven years—their marriage has been loving and strong, and Nichole has become so much a part of our family that, like the rest of us kids, she calls our mother "Mom."

Stepping back behind the security desk, Laura asks how my father is doing.

"Not so well," I tell her as I wheel my suitcase toward the elevators.

"I love your mom and dad," Laura calls after me. "I love your whole family."

"We love you, too," I call back from inside the elevator before the doors close.

All the security and maintenance staff at my parents' condo have been caring and kind, especially Laura and Michelle. And Benjamin, who one day lifted my dad in his arms from an outside bench after he grew too weak to stand, set him in his wheelchair, and pushed him back inside. Lately, my mom has called the front desk a number of times after my dad has fallen and my parents' combined efforts have failed to raise him back up from the floor. Within minutes of my mom's call, someone from security or maintenance is at my parents' door, offering their kind voices and their capable and gentle hands. All but two of the thirty or so condo employees are African American, and about eighty percent of my parents' neighbors in this somewhat luxurious co-op are black as well. I like to joke with my parents, "What is it about you guys that makes other white people leave?" In truth, ever since my parents heard Martin Luther King give his first "I Have a Dream" speech—in downtown Detroit in 1963—they have chosen to live in integrated neighborhoods, and each time my parents have moved into a new community, white flight was already under way.

The elevator rises six floors and opens, and I walk west down the long hall. Nearing its end, I look out the hallway window at the bare, leafless tops of sycamore trees, and beyond them at the side of the Blue Cross Blue Shield building, which has enormous letters painted on it: "Glad to be back home in the D." That's how I feel, too, whenever I return.

My parents' door is unlocked and I step through the small entrance hall and into the large, L-shaped living area, a combination of living and dining room walled by glass on two sides. The river runs beyond the longer wall of windows on my left, the towers of the Renaissance Center loom straight ahead, and the Greektown Casino and Ford Stadium rise beyond the windows toward my right. Even on this gray winter day, the room is brightened by the faint light from outside. Ever since my dad suffered a slight stroke, the Persian rug has been off center, pushed close to the window-walls so that my dad has a wide area of bare floor to manipulate his walker.

My mom steps toward me swiftly, calls out, "An-nie!" and hugs me tight. We are both short: she's five three, I'm five four. My mom used to tease me about being the runt of the family, but she has shrunk three inches as she's aged, her spine contracting through osteoporosis, and so it's my turn to tease. Right now, though, I simply hug her back. Then I cross the room to greet my dad. He is sitting upright in the big leather recliner, eyes open and lucid. Now that he rarely blinks and can smile only with effort—a symptom of his Parkinson's—his huge, staring eyes appear even more prominent and intense. "Hi, Ann," he says when I'm right up close, and his voice sounds clear and fairly strong, not garbled and weak as it often does.

I hug him, then pull back a little, so that I can take him in. "You're looking pretty good," I say. "You're sounding good, too."

"I'm feeling halfway decent at the moment," he says, and I'm surprised at how relieved I am to hear this. Even though I've thought, at times, that I'm ready for my dad to die fairly soon—from a fall or in his sleep—rather than continue to watch him decline piece by piece, I know that once he is gone, I'll wish he were still here.

⊙

On my first night back in Detroit, we eat an early dinner—takeout from Steve's Soul Food—and by the time we clear the table, it's only six but dark outside. Lights have come on in the towers of the Renaissance Center, emerging out of the gray in the distance yet seeming close because of their size: the tallest of the three main towers is seventy stories, twice as tall as my parents' condo. Through the panoramic windows to the right of the towers, the Greektown Casino lights flash pale red and icy blue. "Oh, I meant to go for a walk with you today, Mom," I say. It's one of my goals for the week I am home: to go for walks with my mom and also my dad, taking him out in his wheelchair.

"It gets dark so early," my mom responds, gazing out at the softly lit city. "The day just slips away. But maybe it will be sunny tomorrow, and not too cold. Then we can get your dad outside, too."

"Or maybe we can go to the flower house on Belle Isle," I suggest. Belle Isle, rising from the river between Windsor and Detroit, is only a couple of miles from my parents' condo, and it has an old, magnificent greenhouse made up of six spacious, plant-filled rooms. Strolling in the greenhouse, if only for an hour, is like taking a vacation from winter: you're sheltered from the wind, surrounded by tropical plants and colorful flowers, and the domed glass ceilings amplify the sun.

"Well, the nurse is coming in the morning and the physical therapist in the afternoon," my mom says, "so we won't have time tomorrow. But maybe we can go the day after." She turns to my dad. "You'd like that, Ralphy—wouldn't you like to go to the Belle Isle conservatory sometime this week?"

My dad keeps his gaze on the TV, but he answers her. "Yeah, sure," he says. "That would be great."

Tonight he has what my mom calls a "good" night: he wakes up only four times, instead of six or more, and he sleeps from midnight straight through till four-thirty. I get up with him only once, my mom gets up with him three times, and this night's aide, Isadora, gets up all four times. My dad is no longer disoriented, agitated, or combative when he wakes up, as he was in the hospital after he fell and gashed his head two weeks ago. He's in his own bed and he knows it, with his wife of over sixty years at his side.

⊙

We rise late and have a big breakfast. My mom makes *kaseschnittenli* for my dad, a Swiss dish he loves that consists of ham and cheese melted on a slice of toasted bread and topped with a fried egg. I make oatmeal with pears for my mom and me, plus decaf coffee with lots of foamy milk. Isadora is leaving soon, and she insists she only wants black coffee and a slice of peach bread.

We are still at the table when the outpatient nurse from Detroit Receiving arrives. Yvonna is youngish, in her thirties, with short, straightened hair and a loud and friendly voice. It's obvious that she is fond of my dad, whom she calls "Mr. Zito." It sounds strange to me, and I feel like gently correcting her—"*Dr.* Zito"—even though, throughout my life, I've not often heard him called that. More commonly, he's been "Ralph" or "Ralphy," "Dad" or "Old Man." My brother Dan used to jokingly call him "Pasta," claiming it was an Italian endearment for "Papa." My mom sometimes calls him "Ralphy Darling."

My mom tells the nurse that I am their daughter, and Yvonna considers my face and pronounces, "You favor your father." Then she turns to my dad and says, "So how *are* you this morning, Mr. Zito?"

My dad clears his throat and collects his voice. "Well, if you subtract the fact that I have Parkinson's, I feel like I could jog around the block."

Yvonna laughs, and Isadora does, too. Isadora is from Jamaica, and even her laughter sounds like notes of music.

When it's quiet again, my dad says, "If you discount the fact that it takes all I've got to lift a fork to my mouth, I'm not doing all that bad."

"So—not that bad," Yvonna says, resting her hand on my dad's shoulder. She glances down at the portion of ham, cheese, egg and bread left on his plate. "It looks like you're getting well fed, anyway."

"One of the few things my wife is still good for."

"*Mis*ter Zito!" Yvonna says, gripping his shoulder and giving it a shake. "You are full of spice this morning!"

"Not spice," my mom says; "snakes and snails and puppy dog tails," and I remember the rhyme from my childhood: it was girls who were made of sugar and spice and everything nice.

My dad says something I don't catch.

"You better be nice, Ralphy," my mom warns, "or I'm going to start calling you Staplehead."

"Staplehead!" Yvonna says. "What for?"

"Our daughter was cutting his hair, and she noticed that the doctor left a staple in his head."

"No!" Yvonna says, and she stands straighter and looks down at the staple the doctor missed. "Well, yes, there it is. What do you know."

"We were wondering if you could take it out, rather than the doctor."

Yvonna rubs the staple and the flesh surrounding it as if she's thinking of prying it loose with her fingers. "I'll have to call and get the doctor's permission," she says, "but sure, I can take it out, no problem."

"Oh, good," my mom says. "It didn't seem worth it to go back to the doctor for just one staple."

Yvonna continues fingering the top of my dad's head, squinting down at it. "I can take it out right here, when you're finished eating."

"You can't take that out," my dad says.

"Why not?" Yvonna asks.

"I wouldn't advise it, anyway."

"You wouldn't?" Yvonna asks. She leans over so she can look directly into my dad's eyes. "Why not?"

My dad pauses. We're all watching and waiting. Quietly, he says, "It's the last thing holding me together."

All four of us women laugh at once. Yvonna pushes his shoulder, harder this time, and cries, "Spices and snails!"

"And don't forget snakes," my mom says.

After we all quiet down, Isadora leaves. The rest of us continue to sit at the table as Yvonna checks my dad over. She measures his blood pressure and records it, takes his temperature, and listens to his lungs with a stethoscope. Everything is normal, except that she hears a slight crackling in his back—there's some fluid in his lungs—fluid where there should be only air. She reports this to the doctor over the phone. She also tactfully mentions the staple that the doctor overlooked, and he gives his permission to remove it. Since there is no fever, the doctor says he'll hold off on prescribing an antibiotic at this time to address the crackling in my dad's lungs, which could be the start of pneumonia. Twice last night, my dad coughed up phlegm, which isn't unusual with Parkinson's, but this phlegm was discolored, due to infection and possibly blood. Could this be the beginning of the end? When he was younger, my dad used to call pneumonia "the old person's final friend."

After Yvonna leaves and we clean up from breakfast, I help my mom dress my dad. She can do it alone, but it's easier with two. My dad's fingers can't work buttons or maneuver a shirt over his head or pull on and tie his shoes. He *is* able to hold out his arms to receive the shirt, and he is also able to help us, a little, to pull up his pants. Once he's dressed, my dad sits in his wheelchair ten feet from the TV while my mom retreats to her and my dad's bedroom to get dressed herself. I go out to shop for groceries, taking their car although it's only a short walk down the street, because I'll buy more than I can carry.

I stock up on groceries, then drive over to the CVS on Jefferson Avenue for more "briefs" (adult diapers) and liquid cold medicine, which can be administered through my dad's gastrointestinal tube. By the time I get home my dad's physical therapist, Arnav Patel, has already come and gone. My mom tells me that Arnav says we should put off our trip to the Belle Isle conservatory until he has taught Dad to transfer from his wheelchair into the car. "Oh, too bad," I say, thinking of pushing my dad through the green and flowery rooms, protected from the bitter wind. "It's pretty cold for walking outside today."

"I know, I can tell from here." My mom looks out and down at the shifting tops of sycamore trees through which snow is swirling. Beyond the treetops, the towers of the Renaissance Center are lost in the white-flecked gray air, except for the sign atop the highest column, which spells GM in red neon that shifts to blue, then back to red. The neon letters seem to float freely, disconnected from the structure holding them up, as if GM, which once reigned over Detroit, is today claiming to own the sky.

We eat leftovers from last night's takeout dinner for lunch—I've been here for almost twenty-four hours, yet I haven't made any meals except for helping with breakfast. I have hardly accomplished a thing, it seems. I'm reminded of what my mom told me over thirty years ago, when my daughter was a baby and I complained that whole days went by when I didn't get a thing done. "You're getting a baby done," she said. Now what's getting done is the end of an old man's life.

⊙

My mom has canceled the daytime aides for the week I am here, and on the following morning, as we are finishing breakfast, I mention bringing in hospice for daytime help after I'm gone, rather than paying for private home care as they've been doing. Using hospice would save money because their services are covered by Medicare. I remind my parents what a social worker told us: that a patient no longer has to be on the brink of death to be eligible for hospice care but only to have stopped all curative treatments, and that leads my dad into talking about when his death might occur, and he starts tearing up.

"Sometimes I think I'm really close, that I can't last much longer," he says. "But then I'll feel a little better. I just don't know how much time I have, or what's going to happen next."

When I was younger and feeling discouraged about the ups and downs of an illness, my dad would reassure me: "Recovery doesn't always happen in a straight line." Lately, watching my dad, I've come to see that neither does decline.

My mom, standing behind my dad, lays her hand on his shoulder and says, "None of us knows how much time we have. You just have to live life to the fullest. You might have only a year left. But you could live another five years."

"Oh, no!" my dad protests, firmly shaking his head.

I voice my strong agreement with my dad: "No way does he have five!"

My mom is not stupid; in fact, although she doesn't flaunt it, she has a genius IQ. What my youngest brother and sister have said flits through my thoughts: Mom is in denial.

"Well," she says, "you could live two more years, or maybe three."

"No," my dad says. "Maybe one."

"Remember, Ralphy, when you told me you didn't think you'd see our sixtieth wedding anniversary? And then, on our sixtieth, you said you for sure wouldn't make it to our sixty-first?"

"Yeah, but I've gone downhill since then."

"Well, you have in some ways," my mom agrees. "But you've also made some gains. You've had more energy since the feeding tube was put in. You've rallied, both physically and mentally. And working with Arnav has improved your mobility and strength."

My dad sighs. "I'm still getting closer to death."

"We're all getting closer to death," my mom says.

My dad turns to me. "It's not that I'm afraid to die." He starts tearing up again. "I just don't know when it will come. Am I dying soon? Or not so soon? Sometimes I think I have a month or less. Sometimes I feel as if I won't live another week. Then I'll feel a little better again."

"Don't worry about when it'll happen," my mom soothes. "It'll come when it comes. And in the meantime, maybe we'll see our sixty-second anniversary."

"That's not likely," my dad says.

"You've been wrong twice so far," my mom points out, her

voice hopeful. "Maybe you'll be wrong again." She rests her forearms on my dad's shoulders and brings her face close to his. "Give me a kiss," she says. They kiss tenderly.

When they pull apart my dad growls, "You're such a damned optimist, Rosie." But I can hear the pleasure and love in his voice.

⊙

After we've cleared up from breakfast, we wheel my dad to the closest bathroom, help him out of his clothes and onto the shower chair, soap him up and hose him down. Years ago, I wondered if it would be difficult to bathe my parents when they got old; I feared I would balk at seeing and touching their aging naked bodies. But I've found it isn't awkward; it's simply something that needs to be done, and so I take off my socks and step into the tub, reaching out almost without thinking whenever and wherever my strength and hands are needed. Once we've soaped him and had him stand and sit a couple of times and traded the hand-held nozzle back and forth until he is thoroughly rinsed, he asks us to direct the spray at his head again, so I hold the nozzle over him, and the spray hits his bald dome and cascades down. While he's had several bed baths, this is his first real shower in a week.

Everything is a lot of work for my dad, and all his standing up and sitting back down and getting into and out of the shower has worn him out. After we've finished dressing him, he falls asleep in the big recliner. Again I'm reminded of how the last stage of life is a lot like the first—all the extra sleeping, eating foods that are liquid or soft or cut into small pieces, needing to be lifted and dressed, bathed and changed. But instead of gradually becoming stronger and more capable and independent, as a baby does, my dad is gradually moving in the other direction.

⊙

While my dad sleeps and my mom putters around the house taking care of many small tasks, I start making chicken scaloppini, a fairly complicated dish. This is the way it has always been in my parents' home and even more so since the two of them retired: a great deal of time, energy, and care goes into cooking and eating. And lunch has become the main meal of the day, since if my dad eats a big meal too late, he coughs more at night, and both he and my mom lose sleep.

I cut up onions and mushrooms and sauté them in olive oil. While these gently sizzle, I slice chicken breasts into small, thin pieces, dredge them in flour seasoned with salt and pepper, and brown them in a second pan. Then I stir up a sauce, using the pan drippings, vermouth, and juice I've squeezed from my brother Zachary's fragrant backyard lemons. Meanwhile, my mom has come into the kitchen and cooked some broccoli, and I've added bowties to boiling water. My mom and I take turns stirring and testing the bowties for doneness.

Chicken scaloppini is the sort of dish you should eat as soon as it is finished; it doesn't hold well. When my dad used to make it, he'd bellow from the kitchen so we could hear him throughout the house, "Get to the table! We're eating in two minutes!" If he didn't immediately hear feet on the stairs or other sounds of compliance, he'd shout out our names—"Mike! Arthur! Annie! Dan! Zachary! C'mon, damn it! You need to eat this while it's hot!"

"We're coming, Old Man," one or more of us would answer. And as we straggled in, he'd still be fussing and cussing as he walked around the table, dividing the chicken onto our plates.

I keep the scaloppini covered while we get my dad's medicines ready, and then we wake him, help him from the recliner into his wheelchair, and wheel him to the table. He puts his brakes on himself. Any little thing he can still manage to do, he likes to do himself.

We eat until we're full, leaving plenty left over, something that never happened with scaloppini when we were younger. My mom starts falling asleep right at the table, so I escort them both to bed. While they are napping, I drive to the Eastern Market and buy bread, olives, ricotta, and mozzarella.

When I step back into the apartment, I creep to the open doorway of my parents' room. My dad's face looks like a cadaver's, the skin stretched thin and tight over his skull. My mom's straight white hair has fallen across her face and blended with the sheets, and at first I don't see her; it's as if she's been erased. But then, out of the whiteness, her mouth and chin take shape. They are sleeping soundly, my dad on his back with his arm around my mom, who is on her side and snuggled close, her head resting on his chest. They always sleep this close, their bodies pressed together or intertwined, and as I gaze at them I wonder how my mom will sleep when he is gone.

⊙

Later that afternoon, we are sitting in the living room when my dad suddenly stands.

"Ralphy! Ralphy, where are you going?" my mom says.

I've joked with her that "Ralphy, where are you going?" has replaced "Ralphy Darling" as her nickname for him.

"I'm going to put on some music," my dad says, his voice annoyed and imperious. He's not swaying or frozen but simply standing, as if he's flashed back to a time before Parkinson's.

"Ralphy, your walker?" my mom half demands, half pleads.

I've already jumped up, trotted across the living room, and snatched up my dad's walker with a déjà vu feeling. I've done this so many times. I bring it to him and set it in front of him, but he pivots away from me with a few shuffling steps.

"Dad, c'mon! Use your walker!"

"Ralphy, please!"

I've repositioned the walker so that it's right in front of him, blocking his way. He sighs and grasps it in his hands.

"If you fall again, Dad . . ."

"Now instead of one chickenhawk," he says, "I've got two pecking at me."

"Use your walker," I say, "and we'll stop pecking."

"You try to control my every move. Especially your mother."

"Oh, Ralphy."

"Dad, I think you like to disobey Mom because it's one of your last ways of being independent."

He is looking away from me.

"And at the same time, you order Mom around. You use her as if she were your proxy."

My dad looks at me sharply. "Well, of course I do," he says. "She is."

⊙

On Wednesday morning, I get a call from the acquisitions editor at the university press to which I've submitted my second book. This editor emailed me last week that she was very interested in my book manuscript, but now I'm not sure whether she's going to say she wants to publish it or if she is calling to let me down gently.

Her voice on the phone, as in her emails, is friendly and warm. She asks a couple of questions about my collection, which is made of up love stories, more than half of which are based on my past relationships with men. And then somehow she is saying that she wants to publish it. While she can't give me a definite yes, she is so certain that my book will be accepted by her board that she wants to offer me an advance contract. We talk about the logistics, and by the time we say good-bye, I'm feeling at once dreamy and grounded. After I get off the phone, I tell my parents.

"That's wonderful, honey," my mom says. "Congratulations."

My dad says, "That's terrific, Ann."

My mom's main wish for us kids has always been simply that we be happy; my dad's primary hope is slightly more complicated: he wants us to succeed at something we love. To this end, our dad has always supported our passions, something his parents didn't do for him. He was the first son of Italian immigrants, and his mother decided that he would be a doctor before he was born, and his father put aside part of his wages as a tool and die maker to help pay for medical school. My dad's passion, however, was for playing ball; he so excelled at baseball that he could have played on a college team. But his father pressed him to focus solely on his studies, and my dad set baseball aside. Eight years later, when he finished medical school, he realized that he didn't want to be a medical doctor, so he went on to become a psychiatrist instead. Eventually, my dad returned to playing ball—in the evenings and on weekends, in adult leagues and with us kids. And while he took pride in his work as chief of psychiatry at Detroit Metropolitan Hospital, his job didn't satisfy a deeper need for expression.

For years, he talked about writing a play when he retired, and when he was in his late forties, he decided to develop his singing voice, which was quite good. My dad had just completed his first lesson with a voice teacher, an older woman who had been an opera singer, when my brother Dan's legs were crushed at a summer factory job and amputated above the knees. Besides spending most of his time in the hospital with Danny, my dad lost the desire and ability to sing. When he called to cancel his lessons, he told his voice instructor that whenever he thought of singing, he felt like crying. His teacher told him she understood: after her sister died, she said, she wasn't able to sing for over a year.

My dad never resumed his singing lessons. But after he retired, he began to paint with watercolors. Then, a year and a half later, Parkinson's began to affect his fingers. They grew stiff, slow, unresponsive, unable to control a paintbrush. Still, he continued to encourage and take pride in the passions of his children.

My parents ask more questions about my forthcoming publication. My mom says, "Now you have another reason to live longer, Ralphy. You have to be here next spring, so you can see Annie's new book."

"I'll try," my dad says. "But I'm just glad to know it's going to happen."

○

Later that morning, the nurse returns, and after Yvonna presses the stethoscope to several places on my dad's back, listening, she announces that the crackling is gone and his lungs are clear. A few hours later, my dad's physical therapist leads his exercise regime: my father sits in his wheelchair, obeying the commands Arnav calls out in his meticulous accented English. "Hold your arms out straight, sir. Now lower them. Now raise them up high—as high as you can. That's right. Okay, let's see you do eight reps. One . . . two . . . three . . ."

My dad lifts his arms up and down, following Arnav's instructions precisely. I am making peach custard pies for my husband's birthday, which we'll celebrate here two days from now, and since the kitchen is so small, I am working on the table in the dining room, which is completely open to the living room and only a few feet from my dad and Arnav.

"Now, sir, I'd like you to raise your knees. Right angles to the floor. Okay, lift your knees. Up, down. Higher. As if you are marching." Arnav holds his palms above my dad's knees. "Higher," he says, "higher." My dad tries to lift his knees as high as Arnav's palms. He manages to brush them. "Good," Arnav says. "Keep going. Mar-ching. Mar-ching. Mar-ching."

My dad starts moving his knees swiftly, up and down, up and down, each time hitting Arnav's extended palms as he says, "Ching." If he were standing and steady, he'd be marching down the hall.

"You're really moving fast, Dad," I say, impressed.

"Good job, sir," Arnav encourages. "Keep going. Now rest."

My dad stops lifting his legs and lets out his breath.

"Very good," Arnav says.

"You really can move," I tell my dad. "I didn't know you still had that much coordination and strength."

My dad doesn't meet our eyes, but he seems very pleased—both by what he can still do and by our praise.

Arnav tells him to repeat the exercise, and as he continues to monitor my dad, he asks me what I am making.

"Peach pies, for my husband's birthday. He's driving over here on Friday from the west side of the state."

Arnav nods, smiling approvingly at the two piecrusts, seemingly impressed as well as nostalgic, and I wonder if he's remembering his mother or sister in India, preparing food he now misses. Turning his gaze and full attention back to my dad, Arnav says, "Okay, sir, two more, and then stop."

My dad lifts his knees twice more, smacking Arnav's palms, and then he comes to a decisive halt. After a brief rest, Arnav hands my dad his walker, helps him to stand, and tells him to walk down the hall. The Old Man shuffles along at a fairly good pace, lifting his feet a little higher than usual. Arnav follows behind him. "Turn around now, sir," Arnav instructs, and my dad turns around and starts shuffling back, Arnav spotting him from his left side.

"Dad, you're doing great," I tell him. "And he listens to you really well," I tell Arnav. "When my mom or I tell him to use his walker, he ignores us."

Arnav smiles but doesn't meet my eyes.

"Maybe we should start calling you 'sir,'" I tease my dad. "Would you listen to us then?"

"No."

"Why not? You listen to Arnav."

My dad takes a few more steps without answering.

"I bet it's because Arnav is a guy," I say. "I bet you're just being sexist."

"It's because Arnav is nice," my dad says.

"Arnav's nice, and we're not? You don't think Mom and I are nice?"

"No. You nag me like a couple of chickenhawks."

I turn to Arnav. "He thinks we're nags because we're always telling him to use his walker. But you agree that he should use it all the time, don't you?"

"Yes," Arnav says, grinning. "At this point, yes."

"See, Dad—Arnav agrees with the chickenhawks."

My dad ignores me. Arnav is grinning widely but keeping his lips tightly closed, as if trying to keep from breaking into a full smile. He starts my dad on more exercises.

⊙

After Arnav leaves, my dad falls into a deep sleep. We don't need to wake him for dinner, since all he is getting is Jevity, his liquid food, which my mom empties from two cans into the bag on the IV pole while my dad sleeps in the recliner. As the tan liquid descends through the plastic tubing and then through my dad's G-tube and into his stomach, my mom and I sit at the table and eat leftover scaloppini with a green salad and beets my mom has pickled.

When my dad wakes, he joins my mom at the table, and they play chess. Despite his mental lapses, my dad is still sharp at the game. My mom wins the first match, and the second is a draw. At nine o'clock, we help my dad get ready for bed. Once again, the day has flown by—at least I've gotten the peach pies made, and I've bought the ingredients I need for my husband's birthday dinner. And between my mom and me, we've taken care of the Old Man.

As I'm saying good night to him, my dad says, "Congratulations, Ann." I'm cheered by his mental acuity as well as by his good wishes—we haven't mentioned my forthcoming book since this morning, yet he has remembered it.

⊙

In the middle of the night, I hear something drop—it sounds like a piece of metal hitting the floor. My mom has told me to not get up at night if I wake up, that my dad doesn't need three people attending to him, but remembering how my dad was confused and combative at night not so long ago, I get up to check.

I pause at my parents' open door. Tonight's aide, Emma, has gone back to bed, so it's only the two of them, the bed cranked so that my dad is sitting halfway up, my mom standing beside him, leaning over him. "Oh, did we wake you?" my mom says. "You shouldn't get up, Annie, we're fine. I was just getting Ralphy some cranberry ice, and I dropped the spoon."

"I'm just making sure he's not being belligerent," I say. They're watching me, both of them quiet, my mom smiling, my dad calm and expectant. "If he was," I say, "I was going to kick his ass."

"I'm behaving fine," my dad says, his voice lucid and gentle. "You know your mother—always dropping things." It's true, my mom has always been something of a klutz, although she's now far more physically adept than my once graceful and athletic dad. I walk over to them and hug my dad and kiss his sharp-boned cheek.

"How does the new author feel?" he asks.

"Fine," I say, once again glad that he remembers. Then I tell him, "But I've been thinking about the men I've written about in my book—all my old boyfriends. I was feeling a little bad for them—you know, because I'm exposing them, to an extent. But then, when I woke up just now, I thought: *Mother-fuckers should have known not to mess with a writer.*"

My dad barks out a pleased laugh.

⊙

On Thursday, my sister picks up our brother Arthur at the airport and drops him outside our parents' building. When I open the apartment door, there he is, grinning, long silvery hair flowing down past his shoulders. He's brought one wheeled suitcase plus the satchel in which he keeps his medications, slung over his shoulder. In his free hand, he holds his cane. "Annie!" he says. "It's so good to see you!" He lets go of his suitcase, sets aside his cane, and clasps me to his chest, holding me tight.

Before he started having seizures, Arthur was the most articulate of all of us kids, and besides being a fast and accurate thinker, he was also quick on his feet. He played more stoopball with our dad than any of the rest of us and more backyard basketball with the neighborhood kids. Now, though he is only fifty-six, slightly more than a year older than me, his seizures have caused lasting damage to his legs and his brain, so he always walks with something to assist him, a cane or a walker, and he often speaks slowly and at times loses his train of thought. He is more disabled than our brother Dan, who is quick-witted and funny and, despite his missing legs, incredibly graceful and swift. Yet on good days, using his cane, Arthur can still walk a couple of miles, and his intelligence still often shines through.

Arthur has changed in other ways—he's more emotional than he once was, closer to laughter and to tears, more likely to tell you he loves you, with feeling. I'm not sure how much of this is due to the changes to his brain, but I think part of it comes from his not knowing how much longer he has to live. Any seizure could result in his death, and the toll of repeated seizures means he isn't likely to live to be old. Life, and everything it offers, has become more precious to him, and he especially treasures the people he loves.

This leads him to a tendency to cling. He'll prolong our embrace for minutes, if I let him. I pull away gently, feeling a little guilty, but our parents are waiting for hugs, too. "Mom!" he says, walking into the living room. As she answers, "Hi, Artie, how are you?" he throws his arms around her and sighs. Above them, on a shelf that runs the length of the vast stereo system, is Arthur's ceramic art—thrown jugs sculpted with forbidding and grotesque faces and a variety of objects jutting from them. In the past two and a half decades, he has focused on creating face jugs, an art form initiated by American slaves and later undertaken by southern whites. Arthur has made the genre all his own. Hundreds of his face jugs are in private collections and a few are owned by museums, including the Smithsonian. My parents own several dozen, all on display. Lately, Arthur has begun marking the names of his three kids on the bottoms of his jugs, so that when he dies, they each will have a few of his pieces, either to sell if they need money or else to keep and remember him by.

That afternoon, Arnav is back working with Dad, and Arthur, too, is amazed at how well our dad can move. "Look at you, Dad! You keep that up, you're going to beat me in a race."

"Mar-ching, mar-ching, mar-ching," Arnav calls out. Our dad's face is focused, intent, and he is hitting Arnav's palms with his knees at each *ching.*

⊙

On Friday evening my husband arrives, and we celebrate his birthday with lasagna, garlic bread, and salad, followed by peach custard pie. My dad says it's the best lasagna he's ever eaten, and Murray is pleased with his birthday pie, into which I've poked a handful of candles. We sing "Happy Birthday" to Murray, and, as usual at our family gatherings, there is a lot of talking and joking and laughter.

That night after our early dinner, our dad is watching TV in the darkened living room when Arthur starts asking him about the Selma to Montgomery march, which has been in the news lately because its fiftieth anniversary is approaching. I stop beside my dad's wheelchair to listen.

I had just turned eight and Arthur was nine when our dad told us he was going down to Alabama to march. I remember his good-bye because it was unusual: he spoke to each of us separately rather than all five of us together, and he was extremely solemn. Our dad returned safely from Montgomery, but I later learned that Viola Liuzzo, also from Detroit and the parent of five children, had been killed by racist whites soon after the march was over, and so had never made it back home to Detroit and her family. I realized then why our dad had taken his time saying good-bye, looking into our eyes and being so serious and quiet.

Our dad wasn't involved in the first attempt to march from Selma. That attempt was broken up by Alabama state troopers, who attacked the long column of men, women, and children with tear gas, whips, and clubs. Fifty people were hospitalized, and that day came to be known as Bloody Sunday. I remember Martin Luther King appearing on national TV afterward to announce that they would try the march again, and calling on Americans of all colors and all religions and from across the whole country to join him. My dad and one of his doctor friends, moved by TV footage of the brutally beaten marchers and by Dr. King's call to action, decided to fly down to Selma to march, and also to help treat the wounded if the marchers were attacked again.

Now Arthur and I are two decades older than our dad was when he walked those fifty-plus miles to Montgomery, and while we have learned more about that march and the civil rights movement in the years since, we have never asked our dad about his experience in the Selma march.

I'd remembered our dad being gone just a few days, but now he tells us that the march lasted for five. "Five days?" I exclaim. "You marched for five days?"

He nods.

"And it rained, Dad, didn't it?" Arthur asks. "I was reading about it on the Internet, and it said that it rained several times along the route."

"Yes, that's true," our dad says.

"Did you have raincoats?" I ask.

"No."

"Umbrellas?"

"No."

"So what did you do?" Arthur asks.

"We got wet," our dad says. "It was refreshing, actually. We didn't have any place to shower along the way, and we hadn't brought any extra clothing."

Arthur and I exchange looks, and Arthur massages Dad's shoulders and says, "Five days! I can't imagine you skipping a shower for even one day, Old Man, fastidious as you are."

"Didn't you stay at people's houses?" I ask. "Couldn't you use their showers?"

"We slept in houses that first night, but then we slept in fields, in tents. There were too many of us. We were passing through small towns, some of them nothing more than hamlets."

"Did you get lessons in nonviolence before you set out?" I ask.

"No. But we were all aware."

"What was it like? Was there a lot of chanting and singing?"

"Not at first. At first it was rather solemn. There weren't many people at the start. Only about two hundred."

"I thought there were thousands," I say.

"Only three hundred were permitted to participate at first," Arthur informs me. "According to what I read, the highway was too narrow. When the highway widened to four lanes, they allowed more people to join in."

"That's right," our dad says. "At the start, over a thousand people showed up, but only a couple hundred of us were allowed to march. My colleague and I were chosen in case doctors were needed. And maybe also because I was a Unitarian. A week before the main march began, a Unitarian minister from Boston was killed. That cast a pall over everything."

"Did you know him?" I ask.

"No. He was killed before I got there."

"Did they find out who killed him?" Arthur asks.

"We didn't know at the time. Later they did—three local white bigots. I don't think they ever got prosecuted." Our dad lifts his hand with a concentrated effort and rubs his temple. "The minister who was murdered," he says, "was eating at a black restaurant and hanging around in the black parts of town, and that was against the rules. He was this white northerner, this Yankee, flaunting southern white rules, and he ended up dead."

"And before that there was also a black man who was killed," my mom says from across the room. "And a lot of black people were angry afterward, when the death of the white minister got so much national attention—not only in the media but also in the movement. There were marches and protests across the country after the minister died, but a black man being killed in the South didn't get anywhere near the same notice." My mom hardly ever just sits—she works on a quilt or knits, or she looks through bills or reads the paper or a book. But passing through the living room and hearing us, she stopped to listen, and now she is sitting in the recliner with nothing in her hands. "Do you remember that, Ralphy?"

"Yes," my dad says. "This young black man was killed by an Alabama state trooper during a previous march. He was trying to protect his mother, and she was trying to protect her elderly father, whom a trooper had begun beating for no reason. The young man was unarmed, but a cop shot him." When I look it up later, I find that the grandfather who was being clubbed was eighty-two, the current age of my father. And that the grandson, Jimmie Lee Jackson, aged twenty-six and a deacon of his church, was shot twice in the stomach, after which troopers chased him out of the restaurant where he and his family had taken refuge. The troopers then continued to beat him in the street until an ambulance called by other marchers arrived. He died in the hospital eight days later.

We are all quiet for a minute. My mom is sitting in the big recliner, her head bowed to her empty hands; Arthur and I have pulled up chairs next to our dad's wheelchair. "The police in Selma were extremely vicious," my dad says, "as they were in a lot of places. And ordinarily a police presence of any kind would make me nervous. But right before the march started, Lyndon Johnson ordered federal troops to protect us. And every time I heard a helicopter or saw one pass overhead I was relieved."

"There were helicopters flying overhead?"

"Oh, yes. Constantly."

Our dad tells us that the helicopters, as well as guards on the ground, some on foot and some driving jeeps, followed the whole march, yet in every town they marched through, there were counter-demonstrators shouting, "Niggers!" and "Nigger lovers!" from the sidelines. "I couldn't believe how contorted their faces were," Dad says. "Completely distorted by hatred." In many towns, Dad tells us, there were black people who joined the march for a few miles, then returned to their towns. In the first hamlets the marchers passed through, the people only stared, looking wary. In towns further along the route, they waved, and later on, they joined in, walking along with the marchers.

I'm sitting very still next to my father, awed by his place in the history of our country, surprised that I've never questioned him about it before now.

"How did Mom feel about you going?" Arthur asks.

"We talked about it," Dad says.

"And she agreed?"

"Oh, sure," Dad says. "I wouldn't have gone without her permission."

We turn toward the recliner where Mom is sitting with her legs drawn up beside her. "Mom, did you want him to go?" Arthur asks. "Or did you just go along with it?"

"Oh, I was for it," Mom says. "I thought it was important. But all week long, I was worried and tense. I remember the first day, Sunday, on the way home from church, the car got a flat tire. All five of you were in the car with me, and I didn't know what to do. Zachary was only a baby; he'd just had his first birthday. Mike was the oldest, but he was only eleven. So I drove to a gas station on the flat—I completely ruined the tire and the rim. And then I had a doctor appointment later that week, and the doctor said I had some little thing wrong with me, and I started crying. The doctor was surprised. He said, 'This is nothing to cry about, it's not at all serious.' But I was crying at the thought that I might have to deal with everything from then on alone, without your dad to help me."

Dad looks across the room at Mom and says, "Your mother was braver than I was."

I think this is true. My dad might have gone out in one terrible moment, like Viola Liuzzo, who was shot in the head; or he might have suffered a fatal beating, like James Reeb, the minister from Boston; or he might have died from being shot and then savagely beaten, like Jimmie Lee Jackson, the young deacon. But my mom would have had to raise five children on her own and live the rest of her life without her husband. She would have had to be strong and resilient month after month, year after year, until all her children were grown, and beyond.

We talk some more about the march, and I tell my dad that when I was little, I had a picture in my mind of him walking shoulder to shoulder with King. "So a couple of years later, when I saw photos of the march in a book, I was surprised that you weren't right there beside him."

"No, he was at the front, with the other notables. But I did walk right beside Pete Seeger for a while."

"You did! Did he sing?"

"Yes. And we sang with him."

"What did you sing?"

My dad is quiet, remembering. "One of the songs was 'We Shall Overcome.' Someone would call out the next line, sometimes making it up on the spot. And I made up a line, and Pete Seeger picked it up."

"Do you remember what it was?"

My dad is quiet again. Then he clears his throat. "We shall all have jobs," he sings, his voice hoarse and soft. "We shall all have jobs. We shall all have jobs, someday. Deep in my heart . . . I do believe . . . we shall all have jobs, someday."

Our dad reverts to his speaking voice. "We weren't marching just for voting rights but also for jobs, better housing, decent schools. Blacks wanted the right to vote so they could help to change things."

As I sit beside my dad, I think of how things have changed, for better and for worse. Dr. King would be proud and glad that blacks and whites, together, elected Obama twice, but he would cry, and cry out, at all that remains wrong, in Alabama and in Detroit and across the rest of our country.

Our dad already told us years ago that no one was hurt on this march, and that the only doctoring he had to do was to wrap a sprained ankle. Now we ask him about the speeches at the end of the march. So many luminaries, political activists, and celebrities were there, including some of the best folk singers of the time—and of course, Martin Luther King, who gave a magnificent and moving speech.

"I didn't stay for the speeches," my dad says.

"Why not?" we ask. This was the best part, the crowd grown from three hundred to twenty-five thousand, celebrating their victory.

His voice soft with emotion, our dad says, "I wanted to get home to my sweeties."

⊙

"I won't say he's about to die," Zachary, my ER nurse brother, says six months later, on the phone from California. "Because I've said that before and been wrong. He's a tough old guy, with a strong heart and good lungs. But if he goes pretty soon, I wouldn't be surprised." According to Mom, Zachary says, Dad is sleeping most of the time, difficult to wake, and when he is awake, he's very weak and confused.

I had decided to skip going in to Detroit this month, but

I'm concerned by this news, so I get into my little red Honda and set off.

When I arrive, around noon, my dad is asleep in the recliner. My mom looks frazzled and worried—she looks like she did four decades ago, the other time it seemed she was losing her husband, when my dad was involved in his long affair. Years after that affair was over, when I asked my mom why she didn't leave my dad then, she said she was waiting for him to come back to her. Not that he'd ever moved out of our house—she meant come back into the intimacy they had shared. She believed that if she waited long enough, he'd return. She was willing to wait, she told me, because she'd never loved any man except him.

As we stand above him while he sleeps, Mom says that Dad has gone suddenly downhill. Only a few days ago he was fine, but now he sleeps most of the time, and when he is awake, he's always confused. "Last night he woke up," my mom says, "and he said that he had to go to the wedding of his niece's son. He has just one niece—you know, Bernadine. And her sons are only, what, ten and twelve? I tried to convince him that there was no wedding to go to, but he insisted there was, and that he needed to find clothes to wear. He also said he'd been asked to say something at the wedding, to give a little speech, and he hadn't written it yet. He was really agitated about it. I told him it was past midnight, and there was no wedding, and he got mad at me. He tried to get out of bed. I finally sat on him to hold him down." My mom laughs.

"You sat on him?" I ask.

"Yes. I pinned him. I sat on his chest, with my knees on either side, holding him like this." She holds her arms out in front of her, palms flat, and laughs again. "He probably could have pushed me off. He was really angry. But I wouldn't get off him, and he finally gave up arguing with me and went back to sleep."

I look at my dad, sleeping now, imagining him pushing my mother and hurting her, then getting up and hurting himself. "Where was the aide?"

"Oh, she was in the bedroom with us, trying to convince him that no one would be holding a wedding in the middle of the night."

As if on cue, an aide, a different one than last night, walks in from the back of the house. "This is Jackie," my mom says. Jackie and I say hi and exchange a few words. She's from Detroit, not Jamaica, but like Isadora, Jackie lives in the suburbs, with her husband and young son. In Southfield, she later tells me. Not only whites have left the city.

As I'm settling my things in the guest room, an aide from hospice arrives. Lasheena is here to give my dad a bath, but she can't wake him. "Mr. Zito?" she says loudly. "Mr. Zito, it's time for your bath."

I join her, putting my mouth next to my dad's ear and saying softly, "Dad? It's time to wake up for your bath." He so loves being clean, he probably wouldn't want to miss this chance. I rub my dad's shoulders; I kiss his forehead, then his cheek. But he doesn't stir, he's sleeping so deeply.

"We don't have to wake him," Lasheena says. "I can bathe him while he sleeps."

"You can?" I ask, imagining my dad slipping off his shower chair onto the floor of the tub, wondering how we will fish him out.

"Not in the shower," my mom explains. "Sheena's just giving him a bed bath."

"Or I can bathe him right here in this chair," Lasheena says. "If that's all right."

My mom says it's fine. She gets a sheet, and as Lasheena lifts my dad's right side and then his left, Jackie and I wrestle the sheet under him. Jackie is short and compact like me, while Lasheena is large and strong. I talk to my dad as we move him, telling him what we are doing. He cries out and flinches a little, moaning. He could be dreaming, totally out of it, but I have a feeling that he is semiconscious. "Sheena's going to give you a bath in this chair, Dad," I say. "We need to get this sheet under you." Finally, awkwardly, with a lot of pushing and pulling and rolling, the three of us have positioned the sheet so that it will protect the leather chair from drops of water as my dad is bathed. During all of our moving him around, despite his flinching and cries, he hasn't opened his eyes.

Lasheena bathes only his lower body. Afterward, we decide to move him to his bed. We pull him up to sitting. He still doesn't wake. Lasheena reaches her big, strong arms around his waist, and with one great burst of strength, she hoists him up, pivots, and sets him down on his wheelchair. His eyes are still closed, his face impassive. This time he doesn't moan or cry out or flinch. I wheel him into the back bedroom, and again, with one great effort, Sheena lifts him from his wheelchair to the bed. Then I help her position him on the bed pad and sheet. His head is like a stone, his body is like a sandbag, and his legs are like rubber. But as I adjust the covers around his shoulders, he whimpers, eyes still shut tight, and his body tenses. He bats me away with hands that are strangely curled. I don't recognize his high, pained cries. I have never seen my father less like himself.

⊙

Later that afternoon, the power goes out. My dad is still asleep. It's four-thirty, a humid summer day, but not seriously hot, only in the low eighties. The air-conditioned apartment is around seventy-five degrees. We stick our heads out into the hall. A couple of my mom's neighbors are also looking out into the hall, and they say that, yes, their power is out, too. We turn back into the apartment. "Well," my mom says, "it'll come back on, eventually."

I run water into three of my mom's largest cooking pots, to use for everything from drinking to flushing toilets, since the building's water pump needs electricity to run, and my mom hunts around until she finds a tiny flashlight. Lew, a friend of my parents, phones from his apartment on the twenty-seventh floor and advises us to open the door to the hallway, which is generally cooler than the apartments, but to keep our windows closed because it's hotter outside. Jackie is scheduled to leave in an hour, and she says she'll wait to eat till after she gets home. My mom and I decide to have a "dessert dinner"—cold rice pudding and a Swiss apple-bread dish called *apfel chue*. My dad fell asleep after eating only a few bites of his breakfast and didn't have any lunch, so, at around six, as he continues to sleep, my mom gives him a can of Jevity through his G-tube.

A half hour later, Jackie has left and her replacement, Jolene, is here when my dad, still asleep, moves his bowels. I have gone into the bedroom to check on him, and when I walk up close, I detect a slight foul smell, and then I hear the wet gurgle of more diarrhea exiting his body. I go out to tell Jolene and my mom, and Jolene comes back with me and stands over my dad. We pause. Then Jolene prepares herself for the harder job. As she pulls on latex gloves, I remove my watch. We have to do this carefully, since we have no running water.

I help Jolene roll my dad onto his side, and then I hold him steady, circling his shoulders and cradling his head as Jolene cleans him, wiping my dad with wet wipes, removing the soiled bed pad and sheet, then wiping him again. My mom brings a clean sheet and pad and says that this is the last pad left—the other two are downstairs, still wet in the washing machine because of the power outage. Jolene and my mom bundle up the dirty laundry and stuff it, dirty side inward, into a plastic mesh laundry bag. My dad continues to sleep. We're not sure what to do with the laundry bag stuffed with the soiled bedding. "We could put it out in the hall," Jolene suggests. "No one will steal it," she jokes.

"Oh, no, I wouldn't do that to my neighbors," my mom says, even though my parents' apartment is at the end of the hall, ten feet from their closest neighbor's door.

"I can put it in my car," I offer. Normally, my mom would protest, but now she stands still without speaking, her face blank except for a little tension, her lips parted. "I'll put it in my trunk," I say decisively. "It will be out of the way there until the power comes back on."

"Okay," my mom says. "That will work."

I get up off the bed and find my shoes, gather up the handles of the bag. It's still light outside, but the stairwells are windowless and the emergency lighting has failed—Jolene told me she walked up here without any light to see by—so I'll need the flashlight for the stairs. By the time I find it and am ready to go, Jolene is sitting on the couch in the living room absorbed in her phone, texting. I have the laundry bag in one hand, the tiny flashlight in my other. Jolene looks up and says, "Do you want to take a baseball bat or something? Those stairways are *dark*."

"No, I'll be fine."

Jolene looks dubious.

"The security desk only lets in people who live here, or their visitors," I inform her.

Jolene lets her eyes do a slight roll, and I realize she doesn't take it for granted that all the people who live in or visit my parents' building are trustworthy.

But I'm not at all afraid. I've never felt threatened by anyone in this building in the twenty-seven years my parents have lived here. I go out into the hall with the laundry, turn on the flashlight, open the door to the stairwell, and enter. It is *dark*, as Jolene said, but my flashlight gives enough light. Light flickers from below, and I hear voices. People are trudging up the stairs. We smile and say hello as we near each other. "Do you know how long the power will be out?" I ask.

"No," a deep-voiced man says, "but it's widespread— covers half of downtown."

"I heard most of downtown," another man counters. He is holding the arm of an elderly woman as they slowly walk down the stairs ahead of me.

As I continue to descend, more flickering lights and more people rise into view, walking up. One of these, a heavy-set woman, groans. "What floor do you have to walk to?" I ask her sympathetically.

"*Nine*," she says.

"Huh!" another woman behind her says. "At least it's not nineteen!"

"You live on nineteen?" I ask.

"Sweetie, I live on seven. If I lived on nineteen, I would not be on these stairs."

Laughter rises and falls from below and above.

When I reach the lobby, two elderly women are sitting on the upholstered chairs, one holding a cane and the other with a walker beside her. Another older woman is sitting in a wheelchair with a thirtyish white man holding onto the handles, and I wonder if he is a relative or a caretaker. The white man seems dismayed, but the three elderly black women look dignified and resigned. They are not happy with this, their demeanors say, but they will get through it without making a fuss. Near them on the lobby tables are bottles of water, provided, I assume, by the apartment staff. I consider going back upstairs and bringing these old women some of my homemade oatmeal cookies in case they are hungry, but first I need to go outside with my soiled bundle.

My car is parked on the street, a half block from the building's entrance; as I walk toward it, I stop another of my parents' neighbors to ask if he knows when the power will come back on. "I heard nine-thirty tonight, out here on the street," he says, "but at the desk, they're saying midnight."

Channel 7 News has a truck parked in front of my parents' condo, but they are not filming. A police car, lights flashing, is pulled up onto the median. By the time I've deposited the laundry in my trunk, both the news truck and the police car have driven off. Not far from me are a well-dressed man and woman, sitting separately in their parked cars, listening to news on their car radios with slightly annoyed looks on their faces: it seems they've been sitting there for some time, and their irritation is turning to boredom.

But it's a beautiful evening. The heat of the day has lifted, and most of the humidity has disappeared. A breeze is blowing, stirring the red and white blossoms of the rose bushes planted along the street in front of my parents' building. They are without fragrance, which disappoints me a little, as odorless roses always do—I can't help comparing them to my great-grandmother's wonderfully perfumed roses. Huge and full and of all different colors—red, pink, white, peach, and yellow—they reached, it seemed, ten feet tall, tended by my great-grandmother in the backyard of the apartment house in Queens where she and my grandparents lived and where my dad grew up. These fragrantless Detroit roses are much smaller and less varied in color, but they're still pretty.

I want to linger down here in the breezy street with the sun about to set, but then I have a better idea: I will go back up and bring my mom back down with me. She's strong enough to walk the six flights down and up again. The exercise and the fresh air and the evening itself will be good for her. I hurry back up the stairs to the apartment.

"It's really nice out," I say. "Cooling down a little, but not at all cold. It's breezy, but the air feels perfect."

"Oh, I don't know," my mom says.

"You should get some exercise, Mom. It'll help you sleep better. And it'll be good for you to get out."

"Oh, okay," my mom says. "Your dad's sleeping anyway, and Jolene is here. A walk does sound nice."

As we start down the stairs, my mom reminds me that her left leg gets a little sore if she walks too fast. When I've asked her what the problem is, and if it can be fixed, she has said, "It's just old age. Even my doctor doesn't have a better explanation." She reminds me now of what her doctor told her to do when she walks up and down stairs: lead with her good leg when she's going upstairs and lead with her bad leg when she's going down. Her doctor suggested a slogan she can chant to remind herself how to step: "Up with the good, down with the bad." It's a chant that could be used, it occurs to me, during any kind of march or demonstration; it would work to voice any sort of protest.

My mom starts saying the slogan out loud now as we take the first flight leading down, seeming to relish the double meaning of the words as she says them: "Up with the good, down with the bad." After a couple of repetitions, she is quiet again.

More people are using the stairwell. My mom pauses a couple of times on the stairs to introduce me to neighbors she knows and greet those she doesn't. Then she starts walking down again, chanting twice, softly, as she resumes moving: "Up with the good, down with the bad." Each flight is made up of two sets of stairs, and as we round the corners and head down the flights, I keep trying to walk behind my mom or in front of her when others approach, but my mom doesn't seem to notice when people want to pass her, and she keeps trying to walk beside me, blocking others behind us until they manage to slip around us. I have noticed lately that my mom can get quite dogged about staying in a particular space, seemingly oblivious that she's in my way or someone else's—in the kitchen, in a store, or on the street. Is it because of her cataracts, which compromise her vision? I think it's more likely because she's overtired or exhausted—she is just single-mindedly slogging onward, taking care of her husband and herself, sometimes failing to notice what else is going on around her.

When we reach the lobby, two of the elderly women are gone, probably taken by relatives or friends to places with working elevators or no stairs, but the one with the walker remains, sitting alone, still looking dignified and stoic and as if she will last this out, no matter how long she must wait.

Outside, the light is just beginning to fade—the sun is behind the buildings now—and the breeze, still delightful, is sweeping along the street. It's different than it was out here only fifteen minutes ago, but the same magical quality remains: a mix of temperature, wind, and light that feels like some sort of blessing. I look up at the sky—it's tranquil, yet in motion, a blend of various blues—and then I walk down the street, arm-in-arm with my mom, feeling more like we're sisters than mother and daughter. As if the reins are slowly being transferred to me, so that ultimately we'll switch roles, and I'll take care of her. But for now, it feels as if it could go either way, and it does—we cook for each other, we help each other help the Old Man: my stubborn and precious father, the only man my mom has ever loved. Later tonight, he'll wake up, agitated and confused, and then the following morning, he'll wake entirely lucid, at once lively and calm. *He's back!* my brother Zachary will email to the rest of our sibs, after talking with our dad on the phone. What seemed almost the end was simply an intestinal infection, from which our dad will shortly recover. He'll live another six months before he leaves this world—he'll die in January, on Martin Luther King's birthday, surrounded by our family. But as my mom and I stroll down the street, we don't know this yet.

We walk the length of the long block, past more fragrantless yet pretty roses, cross the street at the light, walk another, shorter block, and start crossing over the Chrysler Expressway. The light is fading minute by minute, and the blues of the sky are growing darker. We'd talked about walking to Greektown, only a couple more blocks away, but as we near the end of the overpass, my mom slows and then stops. "Maybe we should go back," she says. "It's starting to get dark."

My mom is not suggesting we retreat because we are two small, aging women, one mostly gray-haired and one with hair that's all white; she's not suggesting we retreat because we might look weak and be seen as targets. She is suggesting we turn back now because we are the strong ones here, at this moment, in my parents' world, and if we are made weak, if we are robbed and hurt in the process—well, we can't let that happen. So we turn, still arm-in-arm, and walk back over the overpass. We cross that street and the next, then slowly continue down the long, rose-bordered block that fronts my parents' apartment, and enter through the doors in to the lobby, where the lone older woman is still sitting, steady and calm, with her walker beside her. My mom and I step down the hall to the stairwell, and my mom grasps the handrail. As we start climbing the stairs, I join my voice with hers: "Up with the good," we chant. "Down with the bad."

Acknowledgments

Thank you to my writer friends for loaning me your clear eyes and brilliant minds: Andy Mozina, Bonnie Jo Campbell, Joan Donaldson, Glenn Deutsch, Jane Ruiter, Lynn Fay, Heather Sappenfield, and Jim Ray Daniels.

Thanks to the Quilters, with whom I've shared decades of dessert and tea and stories, yours and mine, and also a little needlework now and then: Judy Bowman Anthrop, Lena Aukema, Linda Charvat, Jane Dickie, Leslie Dokianakis, Joan Donaldson, Patty Dykstra, Helen Fortier, Mary Glass, Kelly Jacobsma, Margaret Longshore, Barbara Muller, Krista Dykstra Raffenaud, Kate Lamere Sarfaty, Roxanne Seafort, Robin Tinholt, Mary Van Andel, Fran Poposki Van Howe, Kay VerSchure, and Robin Williams-Voigt.

Thanks to my book club friends: Vicki Rosenberg, Eddie Parach, Larry and Jane Dickie, Jean and Curtis Birky, David and Alison Swan, and Charlie Schreiner. The world needs more dedicated book lovers and great cooks like you folks!

I'm grateful to the Saugatuck-Douglas Interurban Transit Authority for providing me with a steady job for nearly thirty years, as well as with friendship and camaraderie, and now a pension that allows me to write as much as I wish.

I couldn't have hoped for a more talented or kinder crew than everyone at Wayne State University Press: thank you to Robin DuBlanc, Jamie Jones, Emily Nowak, Rachel Ross, Kristina Stonehill, Carrie Downes Teefey, and especially Annie Martin. I couldn't be in better hands.

Thank you, Sheryl Johnston, my dedicated publicist and excellent ally and friend.

Thanks to my stepson Emerson Wierenga Schreiner, artist extraordinaire, for painting the cover art for this book.

Thanks to my entire big family for your steadfast love and support, especially my mother and father, Susie and Joe, my daughter, Cloey, my brothers and sister, Steve, Peter, Kris, Anthony, and Amy, and most of all, my husband, Charlie.

"Up in the Air" was a finalist for the *Missouri Review*'s 2016 Jeffrey E. Smith Editors' Prize.

"Losing It" made the top twenty in the Ghost Story Supernatural Fiction Award Contest for 2016.

"Spin," in a slightly different form, was a finalist for *Southern Indiana Review*'s 2013 Thomas A. Wilhelmus Award and appeared in 2015 in the special Detroit issue of *Transmissions*.

"Lorelei" won First Place for Fiction in 2017 in the Seventh Annual Literature + Medicine Writing Contest and was a finalist for the *Bellevue Review*'s 2018 Goldenberg Prize for Fiction.

"Note to the New Owners" appeared in the fall 2017 issue of *Arts & Letters*.

"Marching" was a finalist in the 2014 *Glimmer Train* Fiction Open and an honorable mention in 2016 for the *Cincinnati Review*'s Seventh Annual Robert and Adele Schiff Awards in Poetry and Prose.

About the Author

Lisa Lenzo is the author of *Within the Lighted City*, chosen by Ann Beattie for the 1997 John Simmons Short Fiction Award, and of the 2015 Michigan Notable Book Award–winner *Strange Love* (Wayne State University Press). Lenzo's other awards include a PEN Syndicated Fiction Award, a Hemingway Days Festival Award, and First Prize for Fiction in the 2017 Literature and Medicine Writing Contest. Her stories and essays have appeared in *Arts & Letters, Michigan Quarterly Review, Sacred Ground: Stories about Home, Fresh Water: Women Writing on the Great Lakes*, and on NPR.